GUNPOWDER
MOUNTAIN

GUNPOWDER MOUNTAIN

A KID CRIMSON WESTERN
BOOK 1

JARRET KEENE

WOLFPACK
PUBLISHING
— EST 2013 —

Gunpowder Mountain
Paperback Edition
Copyright © 2024 Jarret Keene

Wolfpack Publishing
1707 E. Diana Street
Tampa, FL 33610

wolfpackpublishing.com

Cover Illustration by Claudio Bergamin

Paperback ISBN 978-1-63977-613-9
eBook ISBN 978-1-63977-612-2
LCCN 2024937301

for Michael Fleisher (1942-2018)

GUNPOWDER
MOUNTAIN

1

THE SHOESHINE BOY CAME RUNNING TO FETCH me. A dozen or so miners had been drinking in the saloon for hours, singing old-fashioned tunes and leaving coal dust and bacon grease on the furniture. They'd run out of money and refused to leave. I had a contract with the Blood Nugget to boot patrons when they got too boisterous. The bartender, Jericho, had a revolver behind the bar, but firearms were loud and tended to cause a lot of damage to an establishment.

Also, the town doc, Scullard, didn't like dressing gunshot wounds after being stirred from a dead sleep. It made him grumpy, and when he was grumpy, Scullard was likely to amputate a bullet-nicked limb, even just a flesh wound. With the War between the States escalating, the Union needed every bit of silver to finance its military. Cutting off the limbs of scratched miners didn't generate wealth.

Money made the world go around. That's why I tried to stuff as much of it into my billfold as possible. You never knew when a pretty girl like Poppy wanted to be escorted to the latest performance at the opera house. I loved taking Poppy to see the touring singers from Europe in Virginia City, even if I had no idea what information—or what language, honestly—was being caterwauled on the stage. I couldn't have cared less. As long as Poppy held my hand in the dark, I felt content. Her soft neck tasted like rose petals and sea salt, and I wanted to devour her.

But Poppy suspected that I wasn't a good man. She worried I was bent. Forsaken.

She was right to fret.

I pushed through the batwings and into a noisy swelter of cigarette smoke, stale beer, and human odors. I checked my reflection in the giant barroom mirror and, satisfied, scanned the room.

The rowdy men hadn't noticed me. They were noisy and tossing empty shot glasses at the piano player, my friend Chaparral. They were trying to break his concentration as he performed "Come Where My Love Lies Dreaming." What I could make out over the din sounded good, better than his usual keyboard-banging. Chaparral was the type of musician who improved under stress. At this moment, he grimaced as if in pain, sweating mightily through his wool suit.

I raised my arms in the air. "Gentlemen and miladies," I announced to the inebriated miners. "Last call. Time to head back to your coyote holes. There will be ore to process in the morning."

A hush fell over them like a blanket. I had a reputation, I guess, and already a few miners got up from their tables and made for the exit, giving me a wide berth and avoiding eye contact.

There was one table, however, that didn't seem

impressed. Three newcomers. Ugly and angry from a hard day's work in a dark, dirty hole.

Hips cocked, I made a loose fist, studying my cuticles, my other hand on the butt of my gun.

"You can't be serious," said one of the greenhorns. "That there's just a kid."

Chaparral chuckled, which caused the table of miners to turn in their seats to stare at him.

"What's so funny, ebony tapper?" said one of them.

"There's nothing funny about Kid Crimson," said the brassy saloon girl, Verbena, wiping down a table with warm water and white vinegar. "It's just that you called him by his name. The Kid. His arrival means it's time for y'all to *vete, por favor.*"

"Baby-faced boys with clean fingernails don't tell *me* when it's time to go," growled the tallest one, standing up from the table. He grabbed an empty whiskey bottle by the neck, preparing to use it as a weapon. He looked at me with utter contempt, something I was used to. Something that fed the darkness in me and made me feel deliciously alive.

I pretended to spot a sawdust speck on my boot and carefully dropped to one knee.

Meanwhile, Verbena shrugged. "Your funeral. Chap?"

The piano player made the miners jump by banging out the motif of Mozart's "Deus Irae."

Verbena giggled at their reaction, vexing them.

The tall one raised the bottle as if to smash Chap. But I'd pulled my Bowie knife from my boot and tossed it. The stag horn handle clocked the miner's skull with a THUNK.

He went down hard, his face clipping the edge of a table. There was blood and chipped teeth.

His two friends looked at their unconscious, loudly snoring friend, then looked at me in disbelief.

Arms crossed, Verbena shook her pretty head. "What a mess. I'd better fetch Scully."

"You don't mean—no, not the amputator," stammered one of the miners. He donned his cap as if to signal submission.

"Sir," said Chap. "Please do not impugn the services of Dr. Mortimer Scullard, among the first and finest to graduate from the School of Medicine in Laredo."

"Actually, I heard that school trains veterinarians," I corrected.

"Let's go," said the other miner, putting on his cap now. "You grab his legs. We can get him to the boarding house across the street."

His friend nodded. Together they awkwardly, and without a word, shuffle-carried their accomplice out of the Blood Nugget and, hopefully, to a comfortable bed surrounded by fellow wheezers.

After they'd gone, the bar was quiet. The relief was obvious on Jericho's expression. The sun would be coming up soon, and he began inspecting mugs and glasses for damage before plunging them into a steel tub of hot suds. He'd grab some shuteye before the bar reopened at noon. Jericho had landed a job as a firefighter in town, but when he encountered his first blaze, which resulted in many casualties, he immediately retired. The sheer brutality of the incident marked him. He found his role as a bartender, more often than not, gratifying. People cherished him because he poured generously. He appreciated being appreciated.

Pencil in hand, Chap seemed exhausted as he flipped through a notebook. It contained tablature for a composition he'd been working on for several weeks now. He'd graduated from a music school on the East Coast last spring, and somehow thought he'd play piano on his way to the Golden State. He didn't quite make it that far, but he loved Nevada for the solitude it offered, and for the regular payday a burgeoning boomtown barroom like the Blood Nugget guaranteed him. Chap had ambitions to be a serious composer. With construction on the opera house complete, he hoped to debut an original production there before bringing it all the way to Broadway in New York City in a few years. That's where the real money happened, he claimed.

Verbena was a few years older than the three of us and exuded a flirty yet maternal power. A widow, she ran the Blood Nugget with the spirit of an artist rather than a businesswoman. Her best decision was in hiring us. We didn't drink and had obsessions that kept us occupied and distracted from the depravities of our surroundings. Verbena seemed to always possess more affection for me after I cleared out her bar.

She swatted me with a towel, handed me my Bowie knife, and said, "I knew you could shoot. But I had no idea you threw knockout knives. You're getting soft in your old age, Kid."

Returning the knife to my boot, I laughed at this. We'd recently spent the evening of my twenty-second birthday drinking root beer and playing strip-to-our-undies-only poker on the balcony of the Blood Nugget. It was true that I had altered my methods to a degree, mainly so I might continue to secure jobs in Virginia City. The Comstock Lode was fueling the rise of civilization in Nevada. I wouldn't find much work as a railroad and stagecoach agent if I drew guns on anyone that drunkenly misbehaved.

That was the *old* Kid Crimson. The *new* Kid relied on

his reputation as a killer, though just to keep villains on notice. I could easily and very quickly, if necessary, shoot out the lights—from thirty yards or more.

"Do you prefer me soft or hard?" I replied to Verbena.

She laughed and drew close, grabbing my bicep. "I like you like *this*, Kid—just right."

I removed my hat so I could plant a smooch on her forehead.

"You only kiss me when you want information."

"Heard anything about the railroad?"

She smiled, releasing my arm. "Yes, I have. A special visitor will be here in a few weeks."

"Let me guess. Retired bare-knuckle boxer?"

"No." She poured herself a glass of water.

"An American soprano on a tour of the West."

"You're getting, well, cooler."

"Politician?"

"Red hot."

"Ugh," I said. "Not Governor Nye again. His presence is a pall."

"This visitor is more significant. But I don't want to give it to you secondhand. You should ask Ralston. He has it direct. And I hear he has an offer for you."

Ralston was the railroad director in town. He worked with the mines in transporting all the extracted and processed silver to Carson City, where it filled Union coffers to finance a war with no end in sight. Jericho and Chap had health reasons for avoiding recruitment.

I chose draft evasion, and I had reasons for making the choice. Reasons I'd only shared with Verbena. I trusted her with my life. My secrets. My pain.

She would've had my heart too, if not for Poppy.

"I'll have a chat, then," I said. "First, I need rest."

"You can stay with me," Verbena said. Then she blushed and said, "I mean *here*. In the Nugget."

"Thanks," I said. "But I'm more comfortable at my place."

She stayed silent for a moment. She glanced at Jericho and Chap to make sure they weren't listening. Jericho was rinsing plates, and Chap was back to fiddling on the piano, creating ambient noise. Then she insisted: "Kid, that's not a proper place to sleep."

"I know. But it works for me."

She nodded as I scooped my hat. I headed toward the batwings and she said, "You can always have a bed here, you know."

I nodded. Jericho and Chap looked up to wave goodbye.

The piano player took the pencil from his mouth to say, "See you tomorrow, Kid."

"See you, Kid," said Jericho, mid-slosh.

I waved and headed out into the dark and dust-swirling street.

I relied on my peripheral vision, alert for potential attackers. I had made enemies in Virginia City. Friends, too. But people nurtured grudges in a remote Nevada. In a shattered landscape full of shattered lives, violence was the primary mode of communication. Violence was the only language I spoke as a kid, and everything I was reflected this. Sometimes I wondered if I became a gun-for-hire as a way to validate a feral upbringing. I'd have to ask my father about this the next time I saw him.

It had been five years since we last spoke, and I didn't miss him so much as I yearned to interrogate him. With a gun in my hand, ideally.

I reached the undertaker's office and used my key to gain entrance into the storage shed. Grover, the closest thing I had to a *real* father, provided me with a tight yet cozy space, warm in the winter, shady in the summer. It was full of the coal that he often stockpiled to sell as a side business in the winter months. Grover had thrown old wagon-cover canvas over the anthracite to keep me from getting black lung. But it was a superfluous gesture.

As a hired gun in Virginia City, I didn't expect to live long.

I ignited the kerosene lamp before removing my boots. I took off my clothes, folding them neatly and placing them on a stool beside my sleeping area. I picked up Francis William Newman's translation of Homer's *Iliad*, the war poem to end all war poems.

Then I fluffed my pillow and climbed into my wooden coffin, perched on a catafalque and read the part where Patroclus kills Sarpedon, son of Zeus, on the Trojan plain. Then I snuffed the light and fell asleep in charcoal-scented darkness.

2

THE RAILROAD DELIVERED ON A DAILY BASIS what a lawyer friend called "a cornucopia of dainties." I preferred to label them "products of civilization" or "the good things in life." Fattened, grass-fed cattle from Truckee Meadows. Fresh vegetables from Carson Valley. Carved venison from the foothills of the Sierra Nevada. It was dazzling and mouthwatering to observe these victuals arrive at the station in Virginia City.

But what I loved to see most arriving on the trains was the fruit: oranges, strawberries, lemons, apricots, peaches, pears, grapes, apples, figs. Before they were displayed in delectable heaps in the market stands of Virginia City, I'd nab Poppy the best-looking piece straight off a box car and present it to her in a handkerchief for her to inspect with a sly smile.

God, I loved her smile. Poppy illuminated not only rooms, but entire thoroughfares and buildings. The mining companies could've saved money on all those candle lanterns by simply dropping Poppy into the pit, radiating every shaft and pinion. She was more stirring than the morning sun, which at the moment was piercing my eyes as I made my way to the station to chat with Ralston. I pulled down on the brim of my black palm straw hat to mute the rays. I wore my black sack jacket with the top button fastened. Taut black trousers stuffed into my boots and a black waistcoat over a black shirt with a turnover collar and a bright crimson cravat. I didn't look gregarious, but I certainly looked capable, which is a style that impressed potential employers.

If a US senator or a congressman planned to visit Virginia City, my services would be needed. There were a handful of other guns in town, sure, but I was the best, the fastest, the deadliest. Ralston had likely recommended me to someone in Washington, as he'd done before. Although he and I weren't particularly close, we recognized the hidden sensualist in each other. He, too, enjoyed the finer things, the frivolities. We shared a belief that, in a world of gunpowder and mine waste, it was the smallest and most ridiculous pleasures that allowed us to retain our dignity. In other words, Ralston and I got along. He greeted me warmly as I stepped onto the platform.

"Kid," Ralston said, shaking my hand. He looked portly and businesslike in his gray suit and lavender bolero. "I have business to discuss with you. Can we move to the bar for a pancake?"

Ralston knew my weakness. I could never resist fried dough and black coffee at the Griddle of Doom.

"Absolutely," I said. "But first, may I?"

He smiled at this. "Of course, Kid. You know you don't have to ask."

I jogged over to a freight car, plucked a succulent orange from the top of a picturesque mound of citrus, and joined Ralston for a short walk to breakfast.

The Griddle of Doom was busy, but Ralston always had a table reserved. When we had finished tucking into our double stacks and pork sausage drenched in butter and syrup, he wiped his mustache with a cloth napkin and downed his coffee like it was a shot of whiskey. It was an eccentricity that unsettled my stomach. Especially since my own coffee was still steaming in its mug. Everyone was allowed quirks though. Some business-men, it seemed to me, didn't feel they could wait for their mud to cool. They preferred to scald themselves.

"The President will be here in three weeks," Ralston said, before turning his head to cough into the sleeve of his jacket.

I couldn't help but laugh, delicately working a tooth-pick between my incisors. "President of the Bonanza Firm, I think you mean. There's no way that—"

"I mean President *Lincoln*," he confirmed.

I wasn't laughing now. I removed the toothpick and sank back into my booth seat. "Dangerous. And very stupid. There are Confederate sympathizers here. What value lies in such a risk?"

"There's reward in, let's say, strongly and intimately encouraging the mining companies to accelerate their operations."

"Can't the President provide them with, I don't know, *financial* incentives?"

"Absolutely. But nothing inspires like the man himself. He's quite the public speaker, I gather." He signaled the waiter for more coffee.

"Wrinkly son of a gun, too." I sipped my mug like a man who had all the time he needed.

My assessment seemed to irk Ralston. He fidgeted with a cufflink. "Oh dear, I hope we don't have another burgeoning butternut here in Virginia City."

It was a ridiculous thing to say to someone like me. But Ralston didn't know my history in the South and why I had to leave my native state of Georgia. Now wasn't the time to inform him. I wanted to be part of whatever protection detail was being assigned to the Great Emancipator.

"No nuts here," I said. "Just brass tacks. How can I be of service? And how much does it pay?"

The waiter brought over an aluminum pot and refilled our mugs. Honoring the sensitivity of our discussion, Ralston remained quiet until we were alone again.

"The President has a few Pinkertons, plus a number of US marshals," he said. "But we need cunning eyes on the street, a gun who knows what to look for in a town where everything looks, well, minacious."

"I suppose I can do that. How much are you paying? Why you and not the mining companies? Or the feds?"

Ralston shrugged. "The contingent is arriving by rail. You've done exceptional work for me in the past, so I'm willing to pay three times your usual rate."

"You've got your man." I reached across the table, and he accepted a handshake.

"Kid, if you see anything, report it up the chain. Don't shoot first unless the threat is immediate."

People had trouble forgetting my older methodology. "I understand."

He nodded. "The show is being run by Orion Clemens from DC. He arrives in town tomorrow with his brother, a newspaperman. I'll make introductions at the Blood Nugget."

"Perfect."

His face adopted an indecorous expression before he said, "Still wooing the opium nymph, Kid?"

Anyone else and I would've cracked his skull. "Now,

Mr. Ralston. Poppy is a businessperson like all the rest here in Virginia City."

He harrumphed at this. Then he stared at the syrupy crumbs on his plate and said, "Well, I didn't mean any offense. She's a lovely girl."

"You can pay for this one," I said, reaching across again for a shoulder pat to indicate that nothing was strained. Then I donned my hat and rose from the table. "Time to visit the bank."

Ralston cleared his post-meal phlegm as he reached for his billfold. "Thanks, Kid. Be in touch."

Before I could turn away, he added, "He's a phenomenal soul, you know. The President will improve the destiny of this country."

"Oh, I sense the enhancements," I said. "Sherman's neckties are certainly…transformational."

He gloomily absorbed what I was saying, namely that the Union army's destruction of railroad lines in the South was brutal, uncivilized. "War," Ralston said grievously, "is the worst evil. But a temporary one when peace is finally achieved. We must dream of a better future, Kid. For you and me, and for our grandchildren."

"Oh, I'm dreaming all the time, Mr. Ralston."

He smiled. "Scheming, too?"

"I look forward to meeting this Orion fellow."

"Bye, Kid."

I made my way to the bank, but not for security work. I had a thick roll of bills from Verbena that I needed to deposit before they split the stitches in my wallet. I had the clerk write down my balance for me to consider, even though I knew how much was in my account. I had a big sum, but not enough to buy a grapefruit orchard in Sonoma County.

Leaving the bank, I was stepping off the deck stairs

and into the dusty street when I nearly collided with John Mackay, the burly, fiercely bearded Irish superintendent for the biggest mining company at the Comstock Lode. He glared at me, and my body responded without thinking. I pivoted, hand above my pistol. Chaparral called this my "bird of death" for the way my fingers tended to flutter before I drew and pulled the trigger. When I confirmed that the man before me had no gun, I relaxed.

"Mr. Mackay," I said. "I'm sorry for blundering into the avenue. My mind wandered."

"Did it wander from the memory of you rabbit-punching one of my men last night?"

"This morning, actually, sir. The gentleman had overstayed his welcome. If you have a complaint, I'm sure Verbena can explain the circumstances."

Judging by his reaction, Mackay appeared to acknowledge the uselessness of taking up the issue with Nugget management. "Come on, Kid. I need my men healthy, especially the greenhorns, to push deeper into the lode. Having you clobber them for being ornery does me no good."

Mackay was a fair if demanding boss. I knew the detail that he wanted to hear. "The tall one I banged up? You should know that he threatened the piano player with a bottle."

He kicked at the dust. "I appreciate you telling me, Kid. I'll let my team know not to cause any more havoc. Will Verbena allow them back?"

"Without hesitation," I said, knowing Verbena as well as I did. "At the Blood Nugget, sins are long, memories are short, and grudges are drowned with booze."

He laughed at this. "Good to hear. Turns out I'm dealing with another Union revolt, a serious one this time. The miners may get that additional dollar a day for which they've long clamored. Bad for me and others, but great for the establishments in town."

I stayed quiet for a moment. Last year, I had a lot to do with dissuading miners from pushing management too hard on their demands. I was nastier back then. But mine owners like Mackay, with assistance from Nye, got what they paid for when hiring me: unbridled intimidation.

Finally, I said, "Keep me apprised. Major events are occurring in Virginia City soon. A strike might complicate them, and Governor Nye doesn't need complications."

"I certainly will. Well, Kid, I must shove off now to ask the bank for another credit line."

"Getting your men their extra dollars?" I said jokingly.

"No, we need better explosives. DuPont patent B blasting powder will do the trick, but it's pricier than regular gunpowder."

"Sounds like fun."

"Sounds like the end of the world, I'm told."

"I'll listen for it."

"See you. Kid."

"Goodbye, Mr. Mackay."

My boots needed cleaning after so much walking. I wanted to look impeccable before seeing Poppy today. I went to find the shoeshine kid, Ezra. He was waiting for me over by the water tanks. He had arranged a pedestal there he built himself out of old coffee cans and corrugated cardboard boxes and a discarded but intact velvet armchair. He didn't have a customer at the moment, and looked frantic, darting into the street in between wagons to scan in both directions.

When he saw me, he beckoned urgently, so I picked up my pace.

"What are you on about, Ezra," I said.

"It's Poppy," he said, pushing me in the direction of the Sure Cure. "Trouble at her place. Go!"

The orange in my jacket wouldn't survive the journey, so I handed it to him. He stopped nudging to accept the beautiful fruit, his eyes wide with anticipation. "I can have it?"

"Yes," I said, removing my jacket to hang it on Ezra's wobbly coat rack.

He was already biting into the rind as I dashed toward the Sure Cure.

3

Poppy's place was lumped into the unflattering business category of "opium den." This was far from the kind of place my girlfriend operated. Because of the ongoing Civil War, many men endured agony from their physical wounds. Even those who returned from combat without injury suffered grotesque nightmares, constricted breathing, racing heartbeats. Poppy gave these broken souls relief from their afflictions. She sold a special concoction called blackberry balsam, a mix of opium, soothing herbs, and root extract. I never tried it; I didn't need an elixir. I'd coped with night terrors since childhood and didn't care to dampen them. I preferred the wretched company of my demons. I knew them intimately. We were old friends.

I arrived at the Sure Cure right in time for the show. The place smelled of cloying opium vapors and sage, and was dimly lit with candles. I could make out the lanky, upright figure of the town scholar, Sir William Vestrick. He was a British expatriate, veteran of the Arrow War in China, and former schoolteacher from Denver who'd written a book on John Keats. He'd ingested a great deal of analgesic, but the trauma of his wartime experiences incited his nerves. He was drowsily yet aggressively treating customers to a monologue from Tom Taylor's play *Our American Cousin*. The recitation went unappreciated.

Before I could quiet Vestrick, I tripped over someone sleeping on the floor. As I struggled to regain my balance, my vision adjusted. I saw a stocky ore-processing agent from San Francisco stand up from his cot. He attempted to halt the performance by swinging a lamp at Vestrick, who deflected it. Glass shattered. The violence escalated as Vestrick used his cane to crack the silver agent's thighs.

They began tearing the place apart, crashing into the walls and breaking furniture.

Things rarely got out of hand at the Sure Cure. When they did, I fretted for Poppy. She weighed a hundred pounds soaking wet and loved to tussle. She had a temper that stirred her to confront men twice her size. She carried a jade-handled Derringer in her petticoat. I worried she might get stomped to death or have her gun twisted from her grip.

In this case, I saw her in a bright yellow, embroidered silk dragon robe, barefooted. She was a vision no matter what she wore, no matter her surroundings. She came hurrying from the back room where she stored the weapons of sketchy-looking customers. She'd clearly confiscated Vestrick's gun before he became unmanageable.

After the silver agent tripped on a velvet pillow, he got tangled up in some bustle-lace curtains and began flailing wildly, trying to hit Vestrick. By this time, Poppy had jumped on the old man's back. She growled like a tiger and raked his face with her nails.

Vestrick yelled, lurched backward, trying to smash Poppy into a wall to get free of her. It didn't work because I grabbed him by his shirt and dealt him a hard, open-handed slap.

"You need to stop this right now, Sir Vestrick" I said, peering into his dazed features. "Enough."

Clinging to Vestrick's shoulders, Poppy screamed. "Kid!"

Without turning around, I released Vestrick's collar and sidestepped as the mineral agent took a swing. He caught the teacher flush on the chin. Vestrick fell backward onto a sofa, Poppy underneath his weight.

Angry at the chaos, I boot-stomped the mineral agent's shoeless foot. He yelped, falling over into a table full of pipes. Lying on his side, he clutched his injured hoof, groaning in agony.

Then I pulled the dazed Vestrick from off the sofa and slung him into a bed where another Sure Cure customer was sleeping. I needed to check my dear Poppy for damage.

"Flower," I said, gently bringing her to her lovely feet. "How are your petals?"

Smiling, she was happy for my assistance. She drew close, traced my jawline with her delicious little fingers, and kissed me softly on the mouth. She tasted like lemon candy. "Unhurt. Thank you for getting here."

"I have news. May we chat?"

"Yes, darling. But I need another favor."

"Anything."

"Please help me with Sir Vestrick? I'll handle the mineral man."

I nodded. Without a word, I yanked Vestrick to his

feet. Despite getting struck in the mouth, he continued to recite ridiculous lines from the stage drama, but not as vigorously as before.

I couldn't help but laugh.

I brought Vestrick into the back room. After plopping him into a settee, I asked, "Will you comply, my friend?"

He nodded, pupils insanely dilated, the fight in him drained. He let his chin sink to his chest before mumbling, "So much blood."

"Hold still now. You don't want Scullard doing this, trust me." I checked his vitals, pressing my ear to his chest. I heard nothing unusual. Listening for knife and bullet holes in lung tissue was the extent of my medical training. I undid his shirt and, with a candle as a light source, inspected him for wounds.

"Whadja see there," the old man slurred.

"You're not bleeding, sir," I said, buttoning him up again. "All good."

"Not here," he grumbled, attempting to raise his arms and wave me away. "Peking. A river of blood, I'm afraid. Up to our knees."

He was talking of the war between England and China. He'd come to Virginia City to stake a claim, and succeeded. He was wealthy now, but his hunger for opium nearly outpaced his bank account. Sadly, he displayed signs of a serious addiction.

He was trying, at this moment, to push something into my hand.

"Sir Vestrick, I don't require a tip."

"Take it, Kid," he said. "Might be useful down the road."

It looked like the papers to a mining claim.

"Use this dead-end stake," I said, "in a poker game at the Suicide Table."

"Kid." He pulled me into his opium breath, and I thought I might have to slap him again. *This is nothing but dreaming. Let us on by this tremulous light. Let us bathe in this crystalline light.*

"An American stanza," I said, fixing his collar and patting his shoulders. "Poe. Edgar Allan. I didn't know you enjoyed verse on this side of the ocean."

"I love poetry of every stripe and flavor. I don't like *scammers*, you see. An ore-processor is the distillation of a scammer."

"I see, Sir Vestrick."

"Wonderful, you got the paper?" he asked.

"I do."

"I need rest," he said. He lay back on the settee for some shuteye.

"Sorry I had to hit you, Sir Vestrick."

"Forgotten it already," he said, and in a moment, he began sawing logs, entering the realm of a soldier's nightmares.

I thought to shove the claim into his jacket, but perhaps there was something more to it than Vestrick was letting on. So I folded it and tucked it into my shirt pocket.

When I returned to the vestibule, Poppy had already sent the mineral man to his hotel. "How's the old commander?" she said. "Still bragging of having burned the Chinese emperor's palace?"

"He's fine," I said. "Poppy, do want me to ban him from the Sure Cure?"

She shook her head. "It was my fault for not watching him. Too much blackberry balsam is all."

I shrugged. She knew how to run a business, not me. "Well, I should get my jacket from Ezra."

"I'll walk with you."

"I'd love that."

She slipped on her wicker slippers and spoke in Mandarin to her cousin Sing. Together we exited the Sure Cure, strolling into the morning sun and onto the uneven boardwalk. Poppy had the ability to look ethereal and squeezable in the harshest daylight. She had no flaws. She was designed by God. Together we turned heads in Virginia City, because of our interracial romance, and because we looked so good as a couple, like models in a French clothing catalog.

"What's your gossip?" she said, clutching my arm.

"Word has it that the Railsplitter is, well, riding the rails here."

She stopped walking and looked at me. "Kid, what on earth for?"

"To inspire the mining outfits to work harder. More silver means more Union guns."

"Beating picks and shovels into swords," she said, contempt in her voice. Poppy hated war.

"Not everyone here is an abolitionist."

"Let me guess, Kid. They need you to provide security for the President."

"I'm just another pair of eyes."

"I love your dark eyes," she said, flinging her arms around my neck. "I love it when you do dangerous things."

"Poppy?"

"Yes, darling." She kissed me slowly, softly.

"Tell me if you hear anything."

"About what?"

"Anything that sounds...unusual."

"I always do, darling. Remember when I told you about the jealous miner who carted an artillery shell all the way from Fort Churchill? The one who planned to blow up his neighbor's claim?"

"You did," I said returning her kiss, her mouth tasting of lemon drops and lust. "You angel."

A high-pitched voice in the background yelled, "Get a room at the Gold Hill!" Ezra was giggling as he walked up.

We laughed too. I doffed my hat, indicating my agreement while still smooching Poppy.

"Hey," she said, breaking it off. "We should marry in the church before things get serious. Unless you're not." She swatted me with a fan of peacock feathers she carried with her.

"I'm as serious as a heart attack. When is it convenient?"

"This afternoon is perfect."

"Come on, that's too soon, Poppy. Besides, you've given me an idea."

"For what?"

"For sniffing out something that might present a problem. Does your uncle still have those pigs?"

She gave me a confused shrug. "He has so many!"

"The ones that detect gunpowder in the poker rooms?"

"What? That was in his old place. Before it burned down."

"But the oinkers didn't get cooked into crispy bacon."

"No, Kid. They're in a pen behind his laundry."

"Great. I need you to reintroduce me to him."

"He remembers you. It's hard to forget the tall gunman who brought an arsonist gang to justice."

"Fair enough. I'll pay him a call. I need a few hogs with a nose for explosives."

"I'm afraid to ask. So I'm just going to kiss you."

"Kiss away." Her mouth was delicious.

"Kid," said Ezra. Smiling, he presented me with my coat.

In the year since I'd known her, Poppy routinely shared a fantasy of us getting married and adopting Ezra. She liked the boy, and he liked her. They were both orphaned by war, Poppy when the Royal Navy blasted a cannonball through the defensive walls of the city of Canton in China along the Pearl River. Ezra, meanwhile, lost his parents to a Union shell that blasted apart his family's home on Spring Hill Farm. He carried their corpses on a mattress to a neighbor's house, and then that house was smithereened too. He miraculously survived. I loved them both. Too young to be his father, I considered Ezra a sibling.

I'd do anything to protect the two of them, even if it cost me my life. Which wasn't worth much.

"Thanks," I said to Ezra, donning my jacket.

"You weren't kissing so much as yapping," the shoeshiner said. "Something big on its way?"

Poppy and I exchanged a look.

"Big *ears*," she said, touching his left one with her fan.

He playfully slapped it away. "If something is on its way to Virginia City, I should know."

"You'll know," I said. "I'll be the first to tell you." And then I noticed a hulking figure more than twenty yards away. I recognized the intimidating shape and size of the man on his way to the Dead Dice Saloon. Red-haired, six-feet tall, his face a mask of brutal calculation. I couldn't recall from where I knew the man. But I suspected his purpose here.

Ezra followed my stare, swiveling around to see what I saw. Then he said to me, "Want me to find out about that one?"

"No, don't pry. Outlaws are skittish."

Ezra pushed both hands at me with a *pshaw*. "I know all about bandits and murderers, Kid."

"I know you do. Something different about this one. He has bad energy."

Poppy gave Ezra a hug, and the little guy reciprocated.

"Kid wants you to be careful," she said. "Virginia City continues to grow. New folks arrive every day, not all of them good-natured. Some of them bring evil hearts. The music in their heads is sinister."

"Speaking of music," said Ezra. "Chaparral came by asking for you, Kid."

I watched the unknown-yet-somehow-familiar ogre disappear into the hotel and made a mental note to ask the owner who that might be. "Chaparral? He should be composing his magnum opus in the parlor of his girl's living quarters. What's he want?"

"He didn't say. If you have a moment, you're to meet him at the opera house."

I kissed Poppy again, knowing it would cause Ezra to cover his eyes.

"Uncomfortable," he grumbled into his waxy hands.

"Ezra?" said Poppy.

"Yes?"

"How do you feel about being a ring-bearer?"

"You're getting married?" he said, eyes bright with anticipation.

"Kid promised me a wedding. When he's through cleaning up Virginia City."

Ezra kicked at the dust. "Shucks, that'll take forever."

"Ha," I said. "Maybe not *that* long. I'll see you both later today."

Poppy blew me a kiss, but I grabbed her. She squealed adorably as I gave her a real one.

I put her down and said to Ezra, "Rustle up some customers, little man."

He saluted me, then sprinted back to his shoeshine stand.

I headed toward the opera house to meet my favorite piano player. I'd only taken a few steps in that direction, when a chill ran down my spine. I finally recalled the lumbering gait of the man en route to the hotel; his face and name stabbed their way into my mind.

Bad Jace. The most lethal desperado in the West. A man who lived to inflict pain, and who loved to take lives for no reason other than ghastly kicks. Joining a card game with him was akin to playing Russian roulette with a fully loaded pistol.

When we squared off, I'd be sure to have all the aces —to have the pistol pointed between his soulless eyes.

4

Chaparral's girlfriend, a cute blonde Mormon peepstone-gazer named Rosie, had a spinet piano at her shop that he borrowed to sketch his compositions. To hone his chops, though, he preferred to stretch out on the full-scale concert grand that sat untouched between productions on the opera house stage. The manager, Myles Dominick, respected Chaparral's technique even if he was skeptical of my friend's commercial songwriting instincts. In any case, Chap had his own key to the building. Mornings were ideal for the aspiring virtuoso to spend time with a real instrument shipped directly from Paris.

Chaparral sounded much better here than in the Blood Nugget. The opera house had it all—massive stage, yawning orchestra pit, and glorious rigging that made everyone onstage look exquisitely painted. At this moment, shafts of sunlight streamed in from the glass windows, falling upon the pianist at dramatic angles. He seemed so elegantly placed in front of the keys that I hesitated to disturb him as he pounded out a lavish bit of Beethoven.

He heard me creaking up the riser and paused his rendition. Without turning around, he said, "Kid, you have the carriage of a drunken goat." Then he resumed playing.

"You work that piano like a deaf German composer." I was, of course, referencing Beethoven.

He paused again, this time turning to give me his bright expression. "Why, thank you, Kid. You've never heaped such praise."

"You've never let me hear you play in the morning. What's up?"

He got up from the bench and inspected the strings beneath the propped-open top. "I've been commissioned to write and perform an original piece of music."

"Really? Who hired you?"

"Myles. He says an important politician arrives next month, and that the occasion demands a measure of pomp."

I couldn't hold my sigh. "Well, they're not keeping a secret, that's for sure."

He gave up searching inside the grand and looked directly at me now. "It can't be Governor Nye. He doesn't deserve pomp of any kind. What he needs is a punch in the mouth."

Nye had once said something disparaging about Mormon women, an offense Chaparral couldn't forgive, even though he had no plans to convert.

"Chap," I said, "I don't want you injuring those moneymaking mitts of yours."

"Can he really be coming here?"

"Who, Nye?"

"Lincoln. He must be bonkers."

I shrugged. "I've heard of stranger antics from the man."

"I hear that he stores documents in his stovepipe hat."

"Think he has my birth certificate in there?"

"Ha. You know, Kid, Rosie gazed into her peepstone and had a vision."

"What does she see?"

"Bombs falling from the sky." He sat back down on the bench, grabbed the sheet music, tapped the papers into alignment, and returned them to the rack.

"Hailstones?"

"No. Explosives. Incendiaries."

This made no sense to me. "You mean like off a mountain? Ophir Hill?"

"From the clouds."

A meaningless vision. Figment of a vapor-huffing priestess in Apollo's temple.

"How accurate is she, Chap? With the treasure seeking?" To my incredulity, Rosie had a reputation in Virginia City for pinpointing the optimal place for a mine. For a few dollars, she'd peer into an odd stone with a hole in it that she kept in the tearoom where she served refreshments, and tell you where to start digging. A Latter-Day Saint in dubious standing with the church and a widow, Rosie claimed the rock had been gifted to her from Joseph Smith III. It was said that her husband, a member of the Nauvoo Legion, had been killed in the Utah War a few years back. Anti-Mormon feelings were common in Virginia City, but Rosie's peepstone endeared her. She'd steered ambitious men toward riches. And she had Chap to protect her. He had a penchant for girls with Danish ancestry, and while he couldn't shoot the broad side of Noah's ark, he could punch your lights out before you even knew you were in a fistfight.

"Accurate enough to keep people lining up for her advice this morning," he said. "Kid, I hate to do this, but I need to call in a favor. When Ralston commissioned me to write the music, I got a little cocky."

"You gambled away the advance." I took off my hat to rub my scalp.

"And more," he said, his hands above the keys without striking any notes.

"Well, don't worry about it. Verbena will float you a loan. You can bang away for a few extra nights at the Blood Nugget."

He said nothing to this, letting his hands drop.

"Chap, don't tell me you lost it at the Suicide Table."

He lowered his head and pinched the bridge of his nose.

With a sigh, I said, "It's okay. I'll have a word."

"I'm so sorry to have to ask you."

I walked over to him and patted his shoulder. "You've done a lot for me, putting me in touch with Verbena, for instance. I'd be stuck working in the bottom of a mine if not for you. I can ask Grinaker and the Dead Dice Saloon to cool their horses. You'll get your commission back."

"It's not just money I lost."

"What?"

"I gambled away Rosie's peepstone."

"The heck, Chap. You said she saw bombs and there's a line around the block for her visions."

"She saw the future *before* I gambled at the Suicide. She's using a spare rock for the time being."

"She has a *spare*?"

He covered his face with his hands. "Kid, I'm sorry."

"Can she keep relying on the replacement?"

"It doesn't work as well."

"How much longer before they put the screws to you?"

"They gave me a few days. But they're looking for me now, I assume. Rosie and I haven't got enough to cover the loss."

"Chap, they'll break your fingers."

He nodded. Gazing at one of his hands, he slowly made a fist. "Yes, they warned me. Told me that a man named Bad Jace would pay me a visit."

I set my jaw. "I'll visit the Dead Dice and retrieve the stone," I said. "Now do *me* a favor."

"Anything."

"Tell Scullard to meet me at the Suicide Table."

He was momentarily silent. "Seriously? I don't think it's wise to wage war over nonsense—"

"Do it, Chap."

He knew not to argue. Without another word or glance, he stood up, put on his hideous wool jacket, collected his papers, and scuttled backstage.

I unholstered my Colt Army Model 1860 single-action revolver, spun the chamber, pointed it at a weighted sandbag leaning against an unfinished box set. I thumb-cocked and slowly released the hammer. Then I reholstered. The light was so beautiful in this space I didn't want to ever leave. I wanted to bask for a moment in the splendor of a beam of sunlight.

I had dealings with Grinaker's crooked faro game before. Chaparral had given me a reason to rekindle the old Kid Crimson. Chaparral had propositioned a shackled demon stewing inside me, a monster that needed some fun before the President's arrival to Virginia City. This might be the only chance the monster would have to feast in the months to come. More importantly, this might be the only chance Chaparral would have to avoid dying by his own hand. Besides, it would be good to remind people that the old Kid was always a possibility, a looming catastrophe ready to push everyone off the precipice should they not behave.

The Suicide Table was a cursed game deck upon which miners lost everything before shooting themselves in the head for failing to pay their debts. Most of the time, the game ran like any other game where the house had better odds. Eventually, after stretches of meager wins—for the customers—and consistent losses—again, for the customers—the table took its toll on someone with jingle-jangle in their purse. Then a rash of carnage. A miner with a rich vein would grow bold and get wiped out. The agony of financial ruin would be too much; a self-inflicted bullet the only way out. A wealthy production magnate from San Francisco might fall victim next. A cattleman having sold every head in his herd would suffer enormous and complete calamity. In the weeks that followed, dozens of articles appeared in papers near and far, explaining how a table in Virginia City claimed men's lives and condemned their souls to eternal damnation.

Aside from the Dead Dice employees, only Verbena and I understood the truth: The faro dealers at the Suicide Table operated special "gaffed" dealing boxes. These mechanical "shoes" were designed to cheat players, and to the untrained eye nothing seemed amiss. But I had been trained by my father to spot a rotten system, having spent years in pits of vice and depravity—in gambling dens, bare-knuckle boxing lairs, and cock-fighting cages.

I had no urge to clean up a dirty game in Virginia City. That would be like scrubbing the seat inside an outhouse without ever moving the structure and then letting the waste overflow. Besides, the Suicide Table was a draw, luring even my smarter-than-average friends into a deceptive contest. To play at the table and win was something you bragged about.

I wasn't going to upend the table. I'd let Grinaker, a notorious Confederate sympathizer, know that I knew his business was a sham. I'd put him on notice: I'd only tolerate shenanigans if he left me and my friends alone.

I had the anxious knowledge that to reach Grinaker I must first go through the most dangerous enforcer in the West.

That man's name was Bad Jace.

5

I WENT INTO THE DEAD DICE SALOON BEFORE Scullard's arrival. No point in waiting. Besides, the town doctor's presence would confirm Grinaker's suspicion I intended to commit mayhem in his establishment. Despite its crooked table, the Dead Dice was an organized, spotless environment. Even the soiled doves who worked the cribs upstairs bathed regularly and presented well. Unlike the Blood Nugget, the bartenders there wore three-piece suits and waxed their mustaches. At Verbena's place, Jericho poured with a generous hand, ensuring a customer base. He had to, given his competition here at the Dice, young men in crisp jackets and posh derbies appearing ready to prepare the cocktails of your dreams and to defend you in a court of law if necessary. They couldn't fight nearly as well as Jericho or Chaparral, but sawed-off shotguns under the bar made extended fisticuffs unlikely.

Grinaker was standing behind the roulette dealer, observing a haggard, dusty miner, no doubt having just sold his stake in a barren claim, with his friends looking on as he tried to triple his money before leaving town. Grinaker's usual goon, a meathead named Butenhoff, was perched on his high chair, surveying the room from several yards away with his iron on his belt. Aside from a couple of slow-moving poker tables, the action was at the wheel. No sign of Bad Jace.

As I moved deeper into the saloon, I saw Butenhoff eye-tracking me, keeping his thick noggin perfectly still. When I reached the roulette game, Grinaker lit a cigarette. Without looking at me, he said, "Kid, it's been too long. A pleasure to see you again."

"New chandelier?" I said. A fancy suspended gas lamp illuminated this part of the saloon, providing a warm, inviting glow. The Dead Dice was more hospitable than its name suggested.

Now Grinaker gave me his full attention, his eyes hooded under his fur fedora behind a puff of smoke. "You want to compliment my furnishings, Kid?"

"I'm here for my friend Chap."

Grinaker grunted. "Wish your friend played piano at the Dead Dice instead of pounding away in that pus sore of a bar."

"Come on," I said. "Mean to tell me Butenhoff here can't tickle the ivories like a virtuoso?"

Butenhoff didn't reply, content to glare at me.

"Big Bute here," said Grinaker, smiling wryly, "uses his hands for other purposes."

"About that," I said. "I don't want him touching Chaparral for any reason. I'll pay my buddy's debts and you can continue cheating folks with your silly table of death."

As I began to reach for my wallet, Butenhoff slowly raised his scattergun in my direction.

"Don't worry, Mr. Butenhoff," I said, knowing he

wouldn't pull the trigger with Grinaker in the sightline. "I'm merely presenting your boss with money."

"You walk around with a hundred in your billfold?"

I hadn't expected it to be that much.

"Put away your money," Grinaker said. "Let's make an easy arrangement."

"I'm contracted with the Blood Nugget. It's exclusive, I'm afraid."

Grinaker shrugged. "I'd like to pay you for your stage-coach protection. Butenhoff offers plenty of muscle for a place like this, but he gets horse sick."

"Horse sick?"

"It's like seasickness, except it happens while riding a horse."

I looked at Butenhoff, who solemnly nodded to confirm it was a genuine affliction.

"Okay, so he's useless as a stagecoach agent. What is it you're bringing over?"

"Oh, a smidge of entertainment," Grinaker said. "Heard of air balloons, Kid?"

"I have. You require a security detail for silk?"

"It's not the silk that's expensive. We're bringing over a special hydrogen-generating inflation wagon. It costs a pretty penny."

"I read about those wagons in *The Atlantic*," I said. "The Union army uses balloons to spy on Confederate forces. How did you get such a machine?"

Grinaker shook his head, smiling. "I didn't ask Lincoln. My old buddy Jefferson Davis is letting me have the remnants of his own failed balloon project."

A miner had told me the story not that long ago. Apparently, a well-heeled plantation owner from my home state of Georgia had invested in a Confederate balloon, the *Gazelle*, made entirely of women's dresses sewn together. The South had trouble securing pure hydrogen, so the engineers ended up bringing in illuminating gas, the stuff created from coal, that powered the street lamps in Richmond. The project was moved to the James River, which is where things collapsed. Loaded onto a tugboat, the *Gazelle* was intercepted by Union forces, marking the end of the Confederate war ballooning. By that time, the plantation owner had finally perfected his own hydrogen-fueling wagon…but with no silk balloon to inflate.

Grinaker had somehow purchased the wagon from the Confederacy.

"Color me curious," I said. "What are you planning to charge people for a balloon ride?"

"Depends on how much we end up investing," Grinaker said. "And if we get the wagon in good working condition, minus any damage from bandits. I might ask your fiancée for advice on the price structure. She knows entertainment in Virginia City."

I set my jaw but ignored the comment. "Where do you plan on picking up this wagon?"

"It's coming up from Fort Baker in Southern Nevada. You'll pick it up from the Mormons."

"The US Army is there. You're not bringing a balloon inflater through, with or without a Mormon contingent."

"Kid, I'm a businessman. Think I'd tell the bluebellies what kind of wagon it is?"

I laughed. "So you're saying that if I bring you this wagon unscathed—"

"Chaparral's debts are erased." He made a *poof-it's-gone* gesture with both hands but dropped his cigarette. He bent down to retrieve it from the carpet and popped it back into his mouth.

"That's a lot of time on the trail. In three weeks, I

have another job scheduled. How much does Chappy owe you again?"

He waved away the details. "I'm throwing in a fee, plus an advance." He nodded at Butenhoff, who got up out of his stool and went over to the roulette dealer's till.

The oafish bouncer reached in to pull out a hundred dollars, carefully counted out the bills, and organized them into a neat stack before handing them over to me.

"Wow," I said, taking the money. "A generous offer."

"Don't tell anyone. It'll ruin my reputation."

"There was a man that came through here earlier. Ugly, big, and mean."

Grinaker didn't say anything, exchanging a glance with Butenhoff.

"Bad Jace, from the looks," I said. "I can't have him in town while I'm gone. He'll eat our sheriff for breakfast, and our sheriff is an amoral cutthroat."

Finally, Grinaker said, "Bad Jace is doing a job for me."

"What kind of job?"

"He'll be joining you on your journey to Fort Baker."

I couldn't believe what I was hearing "Grinaker," I said, "you're drunk. I'm not riding with a stone killer. Hire *him* to guard the wagon. You don't need me."

"If I send you alone, there's a solid chance you'll bring the hydrogen to Virginia City. You're brains and brawn. But if I send Bad Jace with you, the wagon is guaranteed to arrive."

The idea of traveling with a sack of rancid bear meat like Bad Jace was abominable. But there was no way on earth I'd leave him here to eventually run into Ezra or Poppy or someone else I cared about. And I'd already taken the money. Sure, I'd let Bad Jace tag along, and I'd let him do all the heavy lifting. I'd manage the problem of bringing a Confederate-engineered balloon-gas machine across Union lines with the help of the Mormons, who had no love for the Union. Along the way, I'd manage the most notorious outlaw in the West. Besides, I had an advantage over most people when it came to dealing with Bad Jace. I knew more than anyone on this planet how much of a bully and a coward he was. I'd use this knowledge to my advantage when it came time.

"Deal, Grinaker," I said, extending my hand, and he shook it firmly. "I'm going to need a few specialty weapons, though."

He smiled. "You'll need a horse," he said. "Heard the last one got shot out from under you."

"It happens in my line of work. Shame, because I love animals. Like your Butenhoff here."

The ogre glowered at me, lowering his scattergun.

Grinaker said, "There's an account for you at the hardware store. Procure whatever you need."

"Will do. You realize you'll require a serious amount of silk to fashion a balloon, right?"

"That's why," said Grinaker, his voice slithering, "I hired your fiancée to sew me an envelope with all her Chinese cousins."

At that moment, bespectacled and messily suited Dr. Mortimer Scullard, leather medical bag unfastened with a bandage spool unraveling in his wake, stumbled into the saloon. He cursed mightily as he smashed his hip against a vacant poker table.

"If you have hot water and a sharp saw," he said, emitting an inebriated belch, "I can get the leg off rather quickly."

We all looked at him, then each other, in horror. He looked back at us, though without focus.

"Or just a saw is fine."

———

"FLOWER," I said to Poppy over lunchtime lamb pies in a booth at the Blood Nugget. "You must tell me these things so that I don't look dumb."

"Darling," she said, forking a hot mouthful and chewing. She was ravenous, because lunch was her only meal of the day, a habit in her I couldn't break. "Grinaker hired my cousin Sing for the silk-sewing job. Sing uses my name to secure employment. He thinks it impresses people."

"Well, it does. But I was blindsided, and I didn't like it. His Confederate sympathies are unnerving, and he's far too at ease in the company of killers."

"Killers," said Poppy, looking at me with concern, "like yourself."

I couldn't say anything. She'd told me that she wanted to marry a good, honest man. I was bad, yet I yearned to be good. I was rarely honest with others, but always true to Poppy. I hoped it was enough. I hoped Poppy would settle for me, save me before the curtain fell on my life. I knew the sun was setting on my stint as a hired gun. I'd live a long life as a farmer or die in a hail of bullets in the streets of Virginia City. It would be decided in the coming years, as the town grew into a metropolis or crumbled due to speculation. Riding with Bad Jace to Fort Baker was dodgy. But I wanted to protect Chaparral, Poppy, Ezra, and everyone else, and the only way I'd smell the rind of a grapefruit in my Sonoma orchard was to make money.

Chaparral dragged a chair to our table and sat down. "Kid, you don't have to do this."

"I know," I said, wiping my face with a cloth napkin. "I'm not just doing this for you. There are other considerations. Financial, mainly."

"Promise you'll put a bullet in Bad Jace when he's asleep."

Poppy gasped and used her fork to poke Chap's arm.

"Ouch!"

"Kid isn't craven," she hissed.

"Fine," Chaparral said, rubbing his shoulder. "Wait for Bad Jace to get drunk and fall off a cliff."

"We're not leaving until the day after tomorrow," I said.

"Important meeting?"

I nodded. "With the Secretary of Nevada. A gentleman by the name of Orion Clemens."

"Heard of him. Appointed by Lincoln."

"To do what?" Poppy said.

"Political antics."

"The Orion fellow's purpose," I said after chewing through another piece of gristle, "is to ensure Nevada does what Lincoln wants. And to see that Virginia City continues to produce silver."

"There's a great deal of the stuff in here tonight," Chaparral noted, turning to scan the bar, lined with thirsty miners using their recent earnings to buy whiskey. "Not enough to make anyone wealthy. Just drunk."

"Chap," I said, "I need you to investigate." I pulled from my coat the claim Sir Vestrick had pushed on me.

"This a claim?" he said, inspecting the paper. "Looks worthless."

"Well, go to the Assay Office and find out. This afternoon, if possible. I'll be busy stocking up on provisions."

"You got it. I appreciate everything you're doing,

Kid." He sprung off the chair, returning it to the adjacent table, and headed out.

"This Bad Jace," Poppy said. "Does he enjoy opium?"

"What scoundrel doesn't," I said, pushing my plate away. I didn't like to overeat in case I happened to meet an enemy after a meal. Too much food made me sluggish, woozy. I needed to be nimble, alert. And I was famished for something else entirely.

"I'll give you something you might find useful. Other than a stack of rifles."

I stood up from the table and buttoned my coat. "I want you to give me everything."

"I need a diamond first," she said, extending her gorgeous hand.

I kissed it, of course. And I gently coaxed her out of the booth.

"Kid?"

"Yes, Flower?"

"Why are you so irresistible?"

"It's the darkness inside me."

"Yes," she said. "I want to be swallowed whole by it."

I took her back to her apartment above the Sure Cure, removed her dragon robe and sandals, and licked her tummy button with my wolf tongue.

6

THE HARDWARE STORE, A PLACE CALLED HOUSE of Hammers, was where Virginia City residents bought their lumber, tools, and, more importantly, their weapons. I needed something long range, with knock-down power to make a pursuer—Paiute warrior, Union soldier, Mormon militia member—think twice about following our tracks. The obvious choice was a Sharps big 50 buffalo rifle. It was a hard-to-find item during the Civil War. If Hammers had it in stock, the price would be astronomical, but Grinaker confirmed that I had an account. A Sharps mounted on top of the wagon would make it difficult for anyone to get close. Unless, of course, he had a .50 caliber of his own.

"That's a real gun," Roscoe said, sucking his teeth. He was the store manager, nosey when it came to weapons. He couldn't be blamed for the hem and haw, though. Roscoe had sold many an iron in Virginia City, watching as, minutes later, it was used to kill a louche gambler, soiled dove, or rival miner. I imagined it took a toll on him. "Doing some buffalo hunting, Kid?"

"Considering it," I said, resting my elbows on his countertop, "if my work as a stagecoach agent dries up."

"I believe I have one lying around in the back. I was thinking of taking it to Carson City, selling it to a fellow I know there who's preparing for a hunt."

"Sell it to *me*, Roscoe. I have an account now through Mr. Grinaker."

Roscoe nodded. "Yep, yep. Troubling, but you got a good head on your shoulders, Kid."

"Thanks, Roscoe."

After he headed to the back, I stood up to examine myself in a full-length mirror. Suddenly the sunlight dimmed; the atmosphere changed. There was a horrid smell, like two hogs rutting in a sluice of fecal matter. I turned and watched a gargantuan butcher shamble into the shop, squinting and scanning for threats. His posture was relaxed, because he'd determined my presence. He sauntered toward me, unbothered, working a toothpick in his tusks.

"I sniffed you before I saw you, Mr. Bad Jace," I said. "I'd urge you to bathe before our sojourn to Fort Baker, but I fear there's not enough soap in Virginia City."

Bad Jace smiled, rubbing his fingers on a length of pinewood. "You have a smart mouth, Kid. If you didn't make me laugh, I'd wring your neck."

"I appreciate the affection. Stocking up for our odyssey?"

He shrugged. "Got everything I need. Curious to see what you're putting on Grinaker's tab."

"Here you go, Kid," Roscoe said, returning from the back of the store. He blinked rapidly and his face contorted at the rank odor that had saturated his store in his brief absence. It was so much that his voice went up in register. "Sharps .50 cal. I'll throw in a case of bullets."

Impressed, Bad Jace whistled. "That one kicks."

"Throw in *all* the cases, Roscoe," I said. "It's a long ride to Fort Baker."

"Gun's too big for a slender boy," the reeking outlaw said.

In one fluid yet savage motion, I grabbed the rifle, half-cocked the hammer, yanked open the breech, shoved a round inside, closed the breech, pulled the hammer all the way back, and pointed the rifle directly at Bad Jace. My trigger finger never dipped into the guard.

He took a step backward, toothpick falling from his mouth. His skull clanged against a rack of horseshoes hanging from a hook.

"Lord," Roscoe whimpered, closing his eyes. He covered his ears and braced against a barrel.

"Perfectly oiled," I said, wrenching the bolt to eject the cartridge. I snapped it from the air with my trigger hand, tossed the round at Bad Jace. He fumbled, and it pinged the floor.

He ignored it and said, "Not waiting for you. Leaving at dawn."

"Grinaker know?" I said.

Bad Jace grunted. "Got a little business in Lone Pine. Figure you meet me there."

"That works. You'll have a day's ride ahead of me."

He nodded and, spurs jangling, exited the shop. His rank odor didn't leave with him, however.

I heard Roscoe breathe a sigh of relief as I placed the rifle on the counter and retrieved the bullet.

"Bad Jace," he said. "For years, I believed him to be mythical, a bogeyman for children. But here he was, stinking up my shop and eclipsing the rays of the sun with his massive body."

"He's real. Maybe too real."

"Anything else you need, Kid? My chest feels tight, and I want to ventilate the shop."

"Small boat anchor. And a long length of wire."

"You're in luck. Washoe Lake resident sold me his skiff. Twenty feet, do you?"

"It will. Then I need something to shoot it with."

"Shoot it?" Roscoe said. "What do you mean?"

"Something to send it flying. Like a heavy crossbow."

Roscoe scratched his flaky scalp. "I can sell you one. I don't see how you can—"

"Tether the anchor to a bolt, I'm thinking."

Eyes wide, he grasped the concept. "And you can secure the end of the wire to—"

"My buckboard."

Heading again to the back, he snapped his fingers. "Yep, yep."

When he brought me the crossbow, I used pliers to bend a J hook around one of the bolts and the anchor, fusing them. Then I pointed the bow to the ground and put my boot into the nose-stirrup, cocking the string with both arms. I glided the bolt into the flight groove, raised the bow, and aimed it at a shovel across the store, propped against a stack of drywashers.

I fired the bolt through the shovel's grip handle, the point driving into a support beam. Then I pulled hard on the wire, which tore the anchor loose and caused the flukes to catch the handle.

I had the shovel in my hands in the span of a few seconds.

Roscoe laughed. "You'll be Virginia City's top shovelnabber in no time. What you *really* need to do is point that contraption at Bad Jace, drag him to hell, and leave him there. I can't believe, Kid, that you'd trust him enough to think he ain't gonna backstab you at some point."

I smiled, and recited, "Wise men put their trust in ideas and not in circumstances."

Roscoe was quiet for a moment. "That utterance sounds famous. George Washington?"

"Ralph Waldo Emerson. The *other* Founding Father."

"I hear he likes to swim nekkid."

"Something like that."

I told the old timer to add a sack of Jordan almonds and jelly beans to the total. Poppy had a sweet tooth.

———

WHEN I WAS DONE BUYING a beautiful new sorrel horse and securing him in the livery, I headed to the Blood Nugget. Verbena had a walk-in safe I used to store all my weapons. The place was humming along nicely, minus any sign of hullabaloo, a garrulous energy in the air, with Jericho slinging whiskey for exhausted yet happy miners and Chap merrily tinkling the keys. I headed to the undertaker's office to tuck in early. My odd encounter with Bad Jace in House of Hammers had sapped me. I needed rest before showing up for the dawn's early locomotive bringing Orion Clemens and his journalist brother to Virginia City. Orion had a plan, I assumed, for bringing the President through a territory crawling with Copperheads. I'd have to take notes.

Grover was waiting for me when I walked around the back of his coffin shop. He was smoking a cigarette and watching a stray dog sniff its way through the alley. He was always throwing rocks at hounds to keep them from lapping a puddle of embalming fluid that collected at the edge of his property. He hated to see animals suffer. When he learned that my horse had been killed a few months ago, he was upset and refused to talk to me for a time. He didn't care nearly as much about the buckshot that Scully had to dig out of my arm with tweezers. Grover eventually broke the silence by asking me morbid questions about my Appaloosa, over whom I was grieving more than he could comprehend. Grover loved me, sure, but I confused him with my profession, my inability to settle into a role that might help transform Virginia City from a feral boomtown into a civilized outpost, and my romance with Poppy. Let's just say he wasn't the first father figure to criticize the way my heart felt about a woman who didn't share my same skin color.

Tonight, Grover sat on a stool, his Bible in his lap. I could see he was anxiously contemplative.

"The Lord adores the righteous," he intoned, without opening the book. "But the wicked, those who love violence, he hates with a passion."

"You know," I said. "I was chatting with Roscoe about Emerson earlier."

Grover couldn't help but grin. "You adore that author, Kid, because he asks men to make their *own* bible. The same way you make your own rules."

I didn't say anything to this. Instead, I shared an embrace with the man who'd saved me after a vicious gunfight against a gang of horse thieves plaguing Virginia City two years before. I was seventeen years old. Believing I was invincible, I went right at them in the street, without relying on cover. I'd killed four of them outright, my gun hammering a death song, but the fifth, a seasoned killer, managed to draw his pistol and nearly severed an artery in my leg. I lost blood, enough that Scully had pronounced me deceased. After two teenagers slipped me into one of Grover's coffins, the undertaker noticed I was warm and perspiring. He washed me, and using a medical textbook performed a ligation on a small artery in my upper thigh. He cared for me in my worst moment, bringing me back to full health after I'd been declared a corpse.

It was the old Lazarus trick, and I was grateful. Grover had done far more for me than my own father. My father was a chronic lunatic, a tireless tippler who watched me, at age nine, weighing little more than fifty pounds, bare-knuckle-fight for my life against older boys in rural backwaters for the amusement of gamblers, many of them pederasts. He was the devil incarnate, and I was his son, born in hell. In contrast, Grover gave me succor when I needed it most. He hadn't cured the monster in me, but he taught me I didn't need to be the cruelest man in the world. He taught me I could forgive others, forgive myself, and find love in a world that promised nothing except more pain, disappointment, and tragedy.

He also oversaw the burial of much of my handiwork.

"Grinaker's got his hooks in you, I hear."

"Maybe *I've* got my hooks in *him*. Ever think of that?"

Grover swatted sawdust from his pants. "Not an ideal alliance. The Liberator is coming West."

"I have a few different angles."

"You always do, Kid."

We said nothing for a stretch, then I asked, "What's got you keyed up, Grover?"

"Telegram from Washington."

A disturbing bit of information, and it took me a moment.

"How many?"

Grover closed his eyes, pressed the leather-bound Bible against his forehead. "Fifty coffins."

"Are they coming to inspire the miners or to kill a bunch of them?"

"I don't know, Kid. Maybe the war is moving West. Maybe it's the Revelation."

"End times," I said. "Brother slaying brother."

"He could buy the slaves, set them free. Blockade the South on the water."

"I don't think he wants that."

"On the one hand, I don't think you should leave Virginia City, Kid. Especially with Bad Jace in the saddle next to you. On the other, I think you should leave Virginia City right this moment and never return. Take that China girl with you and go make half-breed babies in Utah. The Mormons have guns and the willpower to wait out the destruction of the United States."

I laughed out loud. "Grover, you've never said that before. You can't wait to be a grandfather!"

He looked bashful. "Well, you've never called me a granddad."

"Come with us. To Salt Lake City. You can do there what you do here. People die everywhere."

"Blegh," he said. "I'm just a janitor. Janitor of the dead. I collect the trash and bury it."

"Does that make me a trashman?"

"Kid, I—" He couldn't articulate his jumbled thoughts, so he hugged me again. I was concerned that he might start weeping, but there was no dampness in his eyes.

I held my surrogate father close under the stars, behind an undertaker's office in a mining boomtown at the edge of America. I only let go when he took the Lord's name, picked up a stone, and hurled it at a mutt that drew too close to a glistening pool of formaldehyde.

7

THE SUN WAS LEMON, THE SKY WAS FORGET-ME-not, and the chuffing engine smoke was as black as the ace of spades. Orion Clemens wasn't at all what I expected when he stepped off the train. He behaved more like an absent-minded college professor than a shrewd lawyer. Clean yet untidy in appearance, he was too shambolic, too self-effacing to advance in politics. Yet he counted many politicians as dear friends, Lincoln among them. He and Ralston knew each other, but it was never clear to me how far back their relationship went. I didn't care much. I was focused on Lincoln's itinerary to and through hostile Virginia City, and how I might protect him. Two things intrigued me, though. First, I was the only security for this meeting; I'd expected to greet a few Pinkertons, but none appeared. Second, Orion's younger brother, Samuel Clemens, was a thorough rapscallion. When I shook his hand, I was repulsed by the clammy softness. However, as we chatted, adjacent to Orion and Ralston's furtive discussions about what locations made the best sense for the President to visit, I was charmed. I realized in those moments that Samuel was a bookworm with a barbarian's perspective on life. He had a knack for selecting suits that flattered him. He had an unrefined yet true witticism for every occasion.

"Mr. Crimson, you seem like someone," he said, within moments of meeting me, "who might shoot a book for being morally decent."

I couldn't help but smile. "I've never fired upon a book. Or an author."

"Well, *I've* certainly felt the desire to put a bullet in both."

"Anyhow, the pen is mightier than weapons, I'm told."

"French satirist Voltaire said, '*To pick up a pen is to wage war.*'"

"Plan on waging war on Virginia City, Mr. Clemens?"

"I won't lie, Mr. Crimson. I see opportunities for carnage."

"What else do you see?"

He turned from me to look down the length of railroad track that stretched toward the horizon. Then he gazed upon the main drag, with the uneven boardwalk of C Street in front of all the saloons, mercantiles, and newspapers—a segregating lane along literal lines of wealth, class, and race. Above C were Stewart, Howard, and A streets; these were the highest on the slope of Sun Mountain, laid out along the original location of the great vein, hosting mansions of the richest mine owners and bankers. Then there was B Street, rife with the superintendents, engineers, lawyers, brokers, and officials. Then D and E streets were down the hill with the

miners' shacks and prostitutes' cribs. The Chinese—with
the exception of Poppy—congregated on I Street, and
then the lowest of the low, the Paiute, existed way down
where no streets were even named.

"An unadulterated wasteland full of wealth, danger,
and exploitation," he remarked.

"*Now* you're selling it. Publish some of *that* and this
town will be overrun by mining outfits."

"Already seems to be the case," he said. "I hear there
are many scribes here too."

"It doesn't cost a fortune to buy a press and start a
newspaper."

"Yes, I suppose spreading misinformation is a cheap
endeavor."

Was he being funny? "I'm absent for a spell with a
stagecoach job. Join us for dinner when I return?"

"I'd love nothing more. Well, I should visit my
employer. Which way to the *Territorial Enterprise*?"

"Take the main strip, then take your third your left.
Then on your right, you'll find the *Enterprise* next to a
den of euphoria called the Sure Cure."

"Thank you, Mr. Crimson," he said, tipping his hat
before ambling toward his newfound battleground.

Orion Clemens and Ralston turned their attention to
me, all of us standing now in front of the bank. My
bosses seemed pleased.

"The rooflines are simple, uncluttered," said
Lincoln's secretary approvingly. "An assassin won't hide
easily in the tops of these structures."

Ralston shrugged. "Still, we need a man on every
terrace."

"About that," I said. "Will there be US marshals?
Pinkertons?"

Orion said, "Oh, they'll be here, staying close to the President."

"We're relying on you," Ralston said, looking at me, "to vet at least five men."

I hadn't expected this. "I'm putting together a team."

Orion studied my response. "You have a few weeks."

It was better to tell them now. "You should know I'm on another job before then."

Ralston removed his hat and propped a boot on the kickboard of a wooden fence. "What now?"

Orion displayed his palms. "Ralston, you assured me—"

"Calm down," I said. "This job might be related."

"Who's it for?"

I hesitated to reveal my clients. It was bad business. "Grinaker."

Orion and Ralston looked at each other, eyebrows raised.

"By all means," Ralston said. "Do it and report back."

"I won't report anything. I'll simply handle it."

"This have anything to do with Long-Haired Bad Jace's appearance in Virginia City?"

"To a degree. There might be something bigger in the works."

"Bigger than the President's safety?" Orion scoffed.

I stayed quiet for a beat. Then replied, "If I'm watching the President, he shall come to no harm."

Ralston nodded and looked at Orion, who seemed satisfied with my pledge.

"However, I required an advance, Ralston. Even Grinaker pays up front."

Ralston theatrically patted the pockets of his jacket, as if to indicate a minor oversight. He found an envelope and presented it to me.

I took the money, counted it, and tucked it into my coat next to the Dead Dice owner's payment.

"This isn't anywhere near enough to hire five more defenders," I said.

"Relax, Kid. I'll give you the rest as soon as you assemble a crew."

"I already know who I want to hire. And they'll each want the same."

"Then Ralston will place money in your account this afternoon," said the President's man.

I shook their hands, sealing the deal.

"Well," said Orion, "I should check into the hotel before we tour the Ophir Mine."

"Be there in a moment," Ralston said.

"Wonderful to meet you, Kid."

"Same."

After Orion was out of earshot, Ralston noted, "The sibling forces are dispatched."

"The younger one is an unapologetic propagandist," I said. "But he possesses charisma at least."

"More so than Lincoln's secretary, yes?"

I changed the subject. "Strange details are coming into focus."

"Like what?"

"Come on, did you think Grover wouldn't tell me? Coffins."

Ralston waved it off. "The government is pushing to hire miners. It's a dangerous profession."

"Where are the Marshals and Pinkertons? I have total confidence in myself, Ralston. I'll annihilate anyone with nefarious intent. But tasking a local gun and his buddies with this job..."

"Yours is not to reason why," he said mockingly, as he backpedaled away, down the dusty street before turning in the direction of the Gold Hill Hotel to meet up again with Orion.

"Mine but to do and die," I muttered to no one.

Were they really planning to lure the President into this wasteland of silver and blood? How many people did they plan to bury to pull off such a stunt?

All I knew for certain was I'd shield Lincoln, as well as my friends.

I took my money to the bank and deposited it into my saving-for-a-grapefruit-orchard account.

———

I CHECKED on my sorrel at the livery, taking him for a trot in the yard. I wanted to get a feel for his idiosyncrasies, but he had none. He was an ideal companion—strong, responsive, even-tempered, near-telepathic. Slowly gathering the reins brought him to a quick, effortless halt. He felt like an old friend, which is why I preferred to splurge on horseflesh, especially when I wasn't responsible for the bill. A marvelous horse was worth any price. I now had a beast to catch up with Bad Jace in the morning, and to run him down like a dog. I readied my saddle with tack, canteens, and ammunition. I made a mental note to stop by Verbena's place to pick up my new weapons. The sooner I left Virginia City, the easier it would be to track the outlaw. But I needed to check in with everyone before hitting the trail.

I lunched with Jericho and Chaparral at the Blood Nugget. They approved of my decision to draft the Niño twins, Alex and Busto, onto my security team. My friends weren't enthused about involving Poppy, but I couldn't in good conscience exclude her from the action. She loved to scrap and was often victorious in her dustups. Plus, she had wiles. Men revealed intimate secrets to her while smoking opium and drinking her blackberry balsam. A potential killer might visit the Sure Cure to steel his nerves before his assassination attempt and spill the entire scheme, giving me time to neutralize him and his accomplices before Lincoln even stepped off the train. Poppy could weave her way through the throng and keep an eye out for a weapon, someone with a crazed gleam in their eye, someone trembling in preparation for a dagger thrust or trigger pull. Or she might blow an assassin's brains out herself with her jade-handled Derringer.

She was the perfect girlfriend in so many ways.

I couldn't eat everything on my plate, so I packed up my leftovers for the shoeshine boy. Ezra was an effective spy. But I couldn't just hire him and hand him a revolver. He was twelve years old. Poppy would be disappointed in me for bringing him into a perilous scenario. I saw no hazard, however, in letting him run his boot-polishing stand during the President's stay. His vantage—equidistant from the courthouse, Assay Office, hotel, and bank —was unrivaled. If he knew my location, he could relay information to me on his lightning-quick legs. Then again, an open gun battle in the street would be difficult for him to avoid.

When I brought him a box of boiled potatoes and beans, he didn't bother with cutlery. He used his hands to scoop the still-warm food into his hungry mouth, smiling at me.

"You'll hit a growth spurt soon," I said, guiltily. "I should start bringing you more food."

"Poppy fried me an entire chicken in a skillet yesterday."

"She's never done that for me," I said.

Ezra laughed, giving me two rapid eyebrow-raises.

He was an orphan, but the Virginia City residents had adopted him. We all felt a responsibility for the little guy. When he showed up, we loved him right away with his babyfat cheeks and his good humor. It was Poppy who suggested he take up the business of shoe-shining, furnishing him with a velvet chair and with brushes, cloth, and polish. Grover built him a wooden platform. Jericho showed him how to add a sense of flair by stomping his foot while snapping the rag. People love to be entertained, doted on. It wasn't long before Ezra began getting the bankers and high-end speculators as customers. He enjoyed cleaning everyone's footwear, though, which was a problem. I had to teach him not to let miners take advantage. They'd promise him extravagant wealth, giving him a worthless claim on a scrap of paper as he scrubbed their ugly gumboots before they met with a soiled dove in the Dead Dice. I instructed him to take coin only—no ore, dust, or documents. I wrote it on a sign for him to display. He had no problem collecting after that, especially when I began hanging out there. Ezra was a reliable source of information too.

"See the outlaw leave this morning?" I asked.

He nodded. "He had a quarter horse and two rifles in saddle scabbards."

"One of them have a scope?"

"What's that?"

"A length of brass that runs along the top of the barrel."

"Yes. Does it help him see?"

"From a distance."

"Who's he gonna shoot?"

"Hopefully not me."

"He dropped something." Ezra handed me a crumpled-up telegram. I studied the operator's script on

Union Telegraph Company stationery. My buddy and security teammate Busto Niño was the operator there. The message read: *Rattlepeak.*

"That a town somewhere?" Ezra said.

"Yes, just outside of Lone Pine."

"That's where you're headed."

I nodded, smoothing out the paper on the edge of Ezra's shoeshine platform, then folding the telegram neatly and sliding it into my coat.

"Kid, can I come with you?"

I shook my head. "Stay here and keep Poppy safe."

"Okay, but you never taught me how to shoot."

"You don't need a gun. Just let Jericho or Chaparral know if someone threatens her."

Speaking of the devil herself, Poppy came walking up to us from her place.

"Don't tell her I said that."

"I won't," said Ezra, winking.

"Kid," she said, looking outright adorable in a tight green floral mandarin gown and green lace Victorian pumps. "Leaving tomorrow?"

"For the Grinaker job, Flower."

"Cover your ears, Ezra."

He looked at her incredulously, then obeyed with a withering expression.

"Look that way," she said. "No lip-reading."

Ezra sighed and spun on his heel. My heart sank. This was my family, if I wanted it enough.

"Stay at my place tonight, Kid," Poppy said, reaching for the curls under my hat. "You can do whatever you want with me."

"No, Flower." I stepped forward, took her hands in mine, and kissed her. "I'm heading out now. My traveling companion, Bad Jace, is up to something."

"Going to kill him like Chap advised?"

I pulled her close by her hips and kissed her lustfully. "Not unless he gives me reason."

"He's given most people in town plenty of reasons, Kid."

"Fortunately for me," I said, "I'm not most people."

8

I KISSED POPPY AGAIN BEFORE SADDLING. I scabbarded my Sharps and grapple-bow and headed toward Lone Pine, knowing I'd need to drift a bit eastward at the edge of Death Valley to inspect the obscure town of Rattlepeak. I pushed my horse at a steady but not punishing gallop along the trail. It was sunset by the time I reached Carson City on the other side of Washoe Lake. The weather was warm, and I expected the temperature to drop. Sure enough, it was almost chilly in June during the last few miles before the moon began to illuminate. Soon, the landscape changed, and the Joshua trees of the northern Mojave began to rise from the desert floor like godless specters. My horse needed rest and water. I stopped at a hidden campsite next to a spring that lawmen had yet to poison in a lazy effort to thwart horse thieves and stage bandits.

After tending to my sorrel, I built a fire and stared into the flames. I contemplated how delightful Poppy felt in my arms. I recalled the taste of her pretty pedicured toes in my mouth, the smell of her sex. She was unlike any woman I'd known before, and I'd known many. Too many, perhaps, but I loved Poppy with an excruciating intensity. I wanted to run away with her the moment I had enough money to realize my dream of being a citrus farmer. Poppy, however, had her own business. I sensed she wasn't eager to give it up or sell it. Her childhood was rife with devastation, hunger. The British military had pushed her to the brink of cannibalism. Her experience with extreme deprivation likely meant she'd never acquire enough money. She saw herself as a medicinal innovator. Who was I to say otherwise? I couldn't understand what she saw in me, other than, of course, my handsome looks and lethality. Sometimes I felt proud of myself for having endured what I went through on my father's plantation. Other times, I believed the experience hollowed out my soul, leaving a walking, talking ghost in finery and irons.

Whatever, I was no shadow. There was a chance I could be redeemed, healed. If not in a church, with Poppy as my white-wedding bride, then maybe in the rows of a grapefruit orchard in Sonoma, basking in the sunlight while pulling apart the red-colored flesh of a Star Ruby and biting deeply.

My fantasies vanished with the sound of snapping twigs beyond my campsite. I rolled over in my blanket for my gun. I pushed dirt onto the fire, extinguishing it and surrounding myself in smoke and darkness. There was a noise, a short, high-pitched cry, the sound a coyote pup makes when it's happy, ready to frolic with another animal.

I laughed so hard I coughed. "Snake, you idiot! You'll get yourself killed out here!"

The Northern Paiute warrior emerged from the gloam, spurs jangling, moonlight on his sturdy face. He wore cowboy clothes—wide-brimmed hat, shirt under a vest, cotton trousers with leather chaps, boots, silk handkerchief around his neck. "I could say the same of you, Tiny!"

Snake and I met three years before under duress when we were twenty years old. We'd been trying to eradicate each other in the pines along the mountainsides of Pyramid Lake. Out of bullets, we used our knives. His shattered against a rock when he had me pinned and I deflected his attack. I punted him off me. When he ran, I threw my Bowie, which just missed his neck before notching inside a tree. He tried and failed to pull it free. I was on him, kidney-punching him so hard that he yelped. He elbowed me in the front teeth, which to this day are too sensitive to bite into a crisp apple. Then a few settlers I'd thrown in with must've spotted Snake. They sent a volley of lead flying that chipped my kneecap before they were mowed down by a gaggle of Paiutes, who somehow didn't see me as I slid down a mountainside. I blacked out; the last thing I witnessed was me collapsing into a bunchberry patch beside a flowing creek. I thought, *Well, it's over for me.* Then I woke up with Snake sitting on my chest, his weight crushing. His blade pressed my throat.

"I've spared you," he said. "So now you belong to me forever."

"This," I groaned in pain, "isn't a Paiute custom, you dog-breathed ding-dong."

He laughed and hopped to his feet. He reached down to grab my hand and brought me to my boots.

Then I took a wild swing at him, missed, and lost consciousness again.

When I came to again the next morning, I was bandaged and blanketed in a wickiup made from willow frames and covered with branches and leaves. I stumbled naked outside the hut. Snake cackled and, indicating my private parts, said, "Tiny, you need breakfast and sacred datura."

Datura was a nightshade that Snake believed enlarged the small penises of white men. I wasn't tiny, obviously. Snake was simply a jerk who enjoyed ridiculing my manhood. I tolerated it, because he taught me how to hunt and fish in the weeks after our skirmish. My father had only gifted me with boxing, wrestling, and killing skills.

Snake was a brother I never had. He wasn't magic or anything. He was helpful to me and eager to teach me things. He eeked out an existence on the margins of civilization, in the no-man's-land between diminishing Indian territories under pressure from settlers and the US government. He'd spent a few years being raised by missionaries in the Las Vegas Valley, but they didn't stay long and returned him to his tribe on their way back to Salt Lake City. Periodically, I'd run into Snake. We enjoyed each other's company. We'd grown up hard and so we shared laughter over life's dark absurdities. In Virginia City, I sometimes donned a mask to cover my viciousness. With Snake, there was no pretense, zero affectation. We were free to be ourselves in each other's company. We trusted each other, because we were too damaged to trust anyone else.

At this moment, Snake saved me from eating tack. He was carrying by the ears a couple of good-size jackrabbits that he'd snared and clubbed. "Let's eat, Tiny. Get that fire going again."

I cleaned the rabbits by lantern light. After heating my blade in the rekindled flame, I hung the animals from a tree, skinning them by slicing the skin around each hind leg, from one foot to the other. I ran my fingers under the skin, creating a loop on the back of the body, in front of the tail. Holding the hind feet with one hand, I grabbed the skin loop and pulled downward, separating skin from the carcass. From the belly side of the rabbit, I bunched the skin and pulled downward. Then I grabbed my knife and cut from the sternum down through each rabbit's pelvis, careful not to nick the intestines. Plunging my fingers into each body cavity, I grabbed above the heart, and yanked until the entrails were removed. I tossed them into the fire and rinsed the meat in the creek that flowed out from the spring. Then I used mesquite branches to skewer and cook the rabbits over an open flame, seasoning with salt that I'd packed.

I cooked the meat for thirty minutes, until we grew famished, weak with hunger. Snake and I didn't wait for the meat to cool. We greedily burned our tongues and lips. It tasted good.

"You're better at outdoor cooking, Tiny," he said, face and fingers greasy with animal fat.

"Thanks, Snake," I said, blowing on my skewer to cool it. "You, too, are better at things."

"Like what?"

"Being a friendly Indian."

He guffawed. "Ever run into that handful of settlers that survived Pyramid Lake?"

This was his attempt at a joke. None of the settlers had gotten through that initial battle. Snake had killed most of them. I made it out alive because Snake believed me to be a powerful warrior.

"Funny enough, I haven't. You know, Snake, I was hoping you might've run into someone out here yesterday."

He squinted at me in the smoky darkness, chewing. "The smelly one."

"His name is Bad Jace. Tangle with him?"

"Didn't want his stink on me. He smells that way because his soul is rotten."

"Headed toward Rattlepeak?"

Snake nodded. "Tiny, are you bounty-hunting now?"

"I'm supposed to do a stagecoach job with him."

"Stealing or defending?"

"Defending. From Fort Baker to Virginia City."

"You should be burying bluebellies by the dozens," Snake admonished. "Instead of chasing dead spirits in the desert. Makes no sense for a Georgia killer like you to be in Nevada. Your family's land, the place of your people, will soon be invaded by insane men, like the one who stole the Shawnee name, Tecumseh Sherman. Grant released him from an asylum to genocide your pecker-wood brothers in the name of freedom. And where are you?"

"My family and my land never accepted me, Snake. They treated me badly. I wander a barren land for a reason."

He snorted. But I saw in his posture that he didn't doubt my misery. He was, after all, out here in the wilderness for a reason, too. "If you slay Grant and Sherman, all Indians will praise you. You know, Tiny, after they kill Johnny Reb, they will extinguish the Indian tribes." Finished with his meat, he threw his skewer into the dirt like a spear. "I'll just have to kill them myself."

"I do know, and I honestly hope you get the chance," I said. "Tell me about Rattlepeak. I've never actually been there."

"It's a nothing spot. Outlaws conduct shady dealings. A white woman runs a saloon there with a murder of aggressive saloon girls. She lets me comb her long blonde hair as she sings a song."

"That all you do with her?"

"Yes," Snake said, slightly offended. "I'm saving so we can run away and be married."

"In what church?" I said, genuinely curious.

He couldn't seem to answer. Finally, he swept his hand dramatically in the air. "The church of the desert. The true house of God."

"I yearn for the same. But there's no church for us, Snake. Not even in the shadows of Death Valley."

I could see I was making him melancholy, so I asked, "So any outlaws worth mentioning?"

"There's a man in the saloon. He has a machine he's selling."

"What's the machine for?"

"Something silly. Balloon trips in the air."

"Hmm. That deal is supposed to occur in Lone Pine."

Snake shrugged. "Not anymore."

"Does he have the machine with him at Rattlepeak?"

"I don't know. If he does, he'd better watch it closely. Obviously, he talks too much."

"What's the man's name?"

"Dobie."

"I'd head there now, but my horse needs rest. And so do I."

"Dobie is a slow, corpulent man. Bad Jace will need to see a soiled dove, I'm betting."

"What if it's your woman? What's her name?"

"Estrella Matero. She's the boss. She doesn't lie down with anyone, and she and her ladies are more dangerous than the rank bear."

"Matero. Thought you said she was blonde."

"She is," he said, reaching into his denim vest to

show me an ambrotype of a flaxen-haired woman. "She's Spanish, her family from Galicia. She's descended from Viking raiders."

"Vikings. Well, I'll be. Come with me to Rattlepeak, Snake. I might land in trouble and need your help."

"Yes, Tiny, but we must rest for a while. We leave at dawn."

He brought out blankets from the saddle of his cream-colored buckskin horse, tethered behind a clump of cholla. He made himself comfortable by the fire. When I was done cleaning up dinner remnants and washing my hands in the creek, I got back into my blanket.

"Never did say what you're doing out here, Snake."

"Looking for you," he said.

I snapped straight up. "How'd you know I was out here?"

Snake laughed. "Because I was hunting, and this Bad Man had an evil odor. I know that where there is evil, Kid Crimson isn't far behind."

I laid back down to rest. "I thought it was the other way around. That bad people followed me everywhere I went, trying to destroy me."

Snake chuckled darkly at this. Moments later, he was sawing logs.

9

IT TOOK US ANOTHER FULL DAY OF BRISK RIDING
to reach the town of Rattlepeak, a glorified whiskey stop
with a stunning mountain backdrop. The only three
buildings on the single street in town were a stagecoach
station littered with abandoned yet functional wagons, a
pueblo-style adobe church, and a sunbeaten saloon that
teetered on the brink of collapse. It was all picturesque
until Snake and I drew closer and heard the sound of
buzzing flies. I couldn't see the insects, which unsettled
my stomach, full of black coffee and stale biscuits.
Nothing was more macabre than flying scavengers
noisily seeking a moist protein.

"Dead body," I said as our horses trotted down the
main drag, nickering and snorting in the cool morning
air.

Snake glared at me like I was dumb. Picking up his
reins, he cantered his horse ahead of me until he reached
the saloon. He dismounted, tethered his buckskin to a
post, and went inside.

I kept a slow, steady pace, scanning the entire area for

whatever—or whoever—was drawing flies. The sound was uncanny, and I soon figured out why. The noise was coming from the water well situated fifteen yards from the church. I guided my sorrel in that direction, but he hesitated, which irked me. Then I remembered he'd ridden hard for two straight days. I stepped out of my saddle and pulled the reins, bringing us closer to the well. I had a horrible thought; Someone had dropped a bullet-riddled carcass down the shaft, blighting the only fresh water for miles.

It was the corpse of a man, slumped with his neck against the stone casing, feet sticking straight out in a V. Blood oozed from his bullet wounds. He had the water bucket in both hands, the rope connected to it and hanging in disarray from the pulley. Clearly the man, a gunshot victim, suffered extreme thirst in his dying moments. In an effort to quench his burning thirst before he died, he stumbled to the well to cool his throat. Then he expired.

I had an ear out for Snake. I tied my reins to a shade structure that sat atop the well and removed a handkerchief from my coat. I pulled the copper pail from the dead man's grip, wiped the edges down, adjusted the rope, and peeked down the shaft before letting the bucket fall into the darkness with a splash.

Then I saw Snake and a blonde woman—Estrella Matero, I assumed—waving from the porch of the saloon. To my horse's relief, I hopped back into the saddle and headed over to get the story.

I stayed on my sorrel and tipped my hat. "Hello, Miss Matero."

"You're the Kid," shielding her eyes from the sun. Her hair was indeed long, blonde, beautiful. Her face was pretty, too. "Snake always talks about you. Could've used you both last night. Men are never close when it all goes sideways."

To his credit, Snake wasn't chastened. "Your buddy Bad Jace is in trouble, Kid."

"What happened?"

"Three Union soldiers and Bad Jace got drunk here for two straight days," Estrella said. "The dead man by the well, Dobie, was alive and having a grand time with them. Until he explained the supposed worth of his contraption on wheels."

"The hydrogen wagon," I said to Snake, who nodded in agreement.

He nudged Estrella. "Tell him."

She sighed, crossed her arms. "He led the soldiers and this man Bad Jace to Rhyolite Cave, where Dobie was hiding the thing. They gut-shot him. He made it onto his steed, galloped here, and expired on top of the well. Men endure a terrifying thirst before they die of lead poisoning."

"Where's his horse?" Snake asked.

"It ran off. And the soldiers and Bad Jace haven't come back this way."

"Figure they're headed to Fort Baker?" Snake said to me.

"They sound like deserters."

"They are," Estrella confirmed.

Snake was itching to track them. "They won't make it to Arizona."

"Hold on," I said. "Why would Bad Jace join in with bluebellies? He has a pile of loot waiting for him in Virginia City if he brings in the wagon."

"Let's ask him," Snake said, saddling up.

"Boys, don't be long. I need help burying this departed soul. He'll ripen quick."

"Tell the bartender to grab a shovel. Where is he anyway?"

"He ran off after the fuss."

"You hire a *woman* bartender while I went hunting?" Snake admonished.

Estrella rolled her eyes, then said to me, "He talks this way, but when the savagery arrives, he's out camping with friends."

I laughed. "We'll bury Dobie on the way back. We'll bring a few more bodies with us."

"Live bodies are better. Especially if they carry coins and crave whiskey."

Snake was already galloping ahead. I gripped the reins. "See you on the other side, Estrella."

"Which side is that, Kid?"

"The civilized one."

"You'll find me before that happens." She didn't sound seductive, but threatening.

"I hope so, Estrella."

WE PUSHED our horses hard for an hour, slowing the pace but never really letting them settle into a trot. Then we watered the animals in the shade of a mesquite cluster at the same creek that returned to the trail several miles later. I could tell Snake was confident we'd reach them. He wore a sinister grin when he was happy about impending mayhem.

"The wheels on that thing," I said after a canteen refill, "make it easy to follow."

"It's heavy," Snake confirmed. "They have four horses pulling it, but they're taking their time."

"Hungover," I said.

Snake nodded.

"We'll be on top of them soon."

"There's a horse that isn't teamed to the stage."

"I saw that. Bad Jace."

"Can't smell him yet."

"You will," I said.

"What I can't determine is if he's with them or following them."

Not knowing concerned me.

We saddled up and followed the tracks. The sun was at its midpoint now, heating us up and lathering our beasts. A dust cloud came into view on the horizon, causing Snake to make a clicking noise and spur his horse forward.

He hastened ahead of me as I pulled the grapple-bow from its scabbard. Noticing that the trail split, with the right path heading straight up an outer canyon ridge, I opted for an elevated vantage to avoid eating dust. I gave a rebel yell and spurred my sorrel, pushing for a chance to get ahead of both Snake and the stagecoach.

I was hurtling now, trying to keep from cracking my face wide open against the anchor-weighted crossbow in my gun mitt. I had the reins in the other. Eventually, I transferred the straps to my teeth so both hands were on the weapon. We were traveling so fast now that when I perceived a rattlesnake coiled smack-dab in the middle of the trail, I spurred again. We went flying over the serpent, overtaking my Paiute friend and the hydrogen wagon rollicking along, three soldiers on top of the coach, oblivious. There was no sign, however, of Bad Jace on his mount.

The soldier in the driver's box had just nipped from a wine bottle when he noticed me in his peripheral vision. He tossed the bottle, yelled at his buddies, and slapped the reins. Now it was a full-on, dust-blown chase across the desert.

As the other two soldiers brought out their irons, they saw Snake coming up fast behind. They took aim, and there was the crack of gunfire. Snake got low, pressing against his mount, but he didn't need to worry. The Union boys were using Starr Army revolvers, slow and clunky, with hammers that required manual cocking. This meant, of course, they couldn't even shoot themselves with what they were pulling on.

It took me a few minutes to get a hundred yards in front of them. I had several seconds before the stage—it was a standard model, the coach chassis replaced with a wooden crate housing a gas generator—reached me. I knotted the end of the anchor wire from the grapple-bow around a craggy sailing stone at the trail's edge, a rock that must've weighed a hundred pounds. The stone had those eerie streaks behind it that suggested it moved in the desert wind, except when someone was watching. Witch rocks, Verbena called them. In any case, I lay flat on my belly like a reptile between two creosote bushes and had the crossbow ready as the stage approached.

It rolled right into my line of sight. From a few yards away, I fired the flared boat anchor into the back right wheel, shattering a spoke but snagging it nonetheless. The weight of the sailing stone nearly tipped the wagon with its sharp, sudden drag. There was enough momentum that the cart stayed upright—until the stone, trawling the trail dirt, got caught up in the base of a barber pole-size Joshua tree, which ripped the wheel right off the spoke. The left rear end of the stage slammed into the sand with terrific force, kicking up a dust geyser that made Snake hoot with joy as the two soldiers flew off the baggage roof, their bodies smashing into the dirt.

The man riding whip was a nincompoop, pushing the horses to drag the coach despite its missing wheel. It was pathetic to watch; a child in bare feet could've gone faster. I considered clubbing him unconscious right then and there. Instead, I ran in the opposite direction, to keep Snake from killing the soldiers outright before I could interview them.

When I reached him on foot, Snake, blade in hand, was already standing over one, who'd broken his leg from the impact of getting thrown from a wagon. Snake's people didn't scalp, but he knew whites couldn't tell one tribe from another, so he used fear to get answers. The other bluebelly was frozen in the dust, neck broken.

"Where's Bad Jace?"

"No idea," the broken-legged soldier said, his face acne-ravaged. "He took off when we claimed the machine."

"You mean stole it," I said.

Clutching and rubbing his limb, the unarmed soldier shook his head. "No, sir. Archer won it square in a poker game."

"There's no way that Dobie fellow gambled away a hydrogen generator."

"Well, he did. We're taking it back to Fort Baker so we can be reinstated."

"They don't reinstate deserters," Snake said, grabbing the soldier's hair and readying his knife.

"Wait," I said. "Soldier Blue, did you get a look at this machine?"

He thought about it for a moment. "No, sir."

"He's not going anywhere," I said to Snake. "Let's examine the contents."

We looked in the direction of the wagon, which came to a halt, horses exhausted and unable to drag the weight any further. The soldier who'd been driving leaped from the stage and ran toward a garden of Joshua trees, crouching low and stumbling amid uneven terrain.

Snake raised his Henry repeating rifle, thought better of it. "Waste of ammo."

"He's looking to get bit by a Gila. Come on."

When we reached the hydrogen wagon, I nudged the crate and heard a lot of clanking inside.

"Is it broken?" Snake said.

"Shoot the padlock off."

He took a step back, aimed his rifle barrel, and blasted the iron bolt.

I used the butt end of my crossbow to pry open the slats. Snake pitched in with his bare hands.

Suddenly, a fountain of horseshoes and ball bearings and old belt buckles started pouring out, all of that metal clanging like an alarm.

Once the noise ceased and the crate had emptied, I said, "It appears that Bad Jace has the real machine somewhere. I'm thinking Lone Pine."

"Due east," Snake said. "If we hurry, we'll reach it before sunfall." Then he placed his fingers in his mouth and whistled loudly for his horse, which came running over to us.

My sorrel, meanwhile, stood dumbly over where I had snared the stagecoach wheel, chewing on some burro-weed. All the commotion hadn't impressed him. Maybe he was deaf.

"Can you teach my horse to do that?" I said to Snake.

"You're the one who needs teaching."

"Leave the soldiers alone, Snake. You have a terrible gleam in your eyes."

He shrugged. "One is dead, another has a shattered leg, and the other will be dead soon."

On cue, there was a scream, as if the soldier traipsing through the Joshua trees had been bitten by something fierce, poisonous.

"The desert," I said, "can be an inhospitable place."

10

"KID," SNAKE SAID. "SMELL SOMETHING?"

Suddenly, there was the boom of a Winchester. Then Snake went to the ground, clutching his neck. We instantly knew where the shooter had vantage, so we scrambled behind the fake hydrogen wagon for cover before the second shot splintered the wooden brake lever.

"I'm hit, Kid," Snake growled.

"How bad is it?"

He was stoic and composed as he removed his blood-saturated hand. I could see that the damage was all meat, no arteries severed. I placed his hand back on his wound and told him to keep applying pressure. There was now little chance he'd be able to help me. Pinned down by a rifle, we'd have to wait out Bad Jace. There was no other cover to shield me. With my knife, I sliced the front panel from his vest to improvise a tourniquet.

"Left arm," I said. "Raise it and touch your head." I wrapped the cloth tightly under the armpit then his

neck, then I slipped his hand off the wound. I was careful
not to cut off his airway.

"I feel stupid. Give me my rifle so I can shoot back."

"You won't hit anything. He's up on that ridge, too
far away for us to return fire with pistols."

"Tiny, why'd he shoot me first?"

"Obviously, you're the dangerous one."

"Definitely bigger."

"In terms of weight, yes."

"It's all below the belt, fortunately."

"Just like your mama."

Bad Jace boomed the Winchester again, killing one of
the team horses. This spooked the others. They began
slowly pulling the stage down the trail, despite the
weight of a horse carcass dragging across the dirt,
despite the harness straps and tugs getting tangled under
their hooves and under the wheels. Bad Jace got off
another round, missing the horses but crushing the other
rear wheel causing the rear of the carriage to smack the
dirt. Still, things were in motion.

Bad Jace fired again, killing the deserter who'd been
trying to crawl toward a creosote bush for cover.

We'd just begun to crouch, moving with the wagon to
avoid getting bullet-smashed, when there was a deafening, reverberating wallop of a cannon. With the help of
several saloon ladies and two horses, Estrella had
wheeled it over and around the bend in the trail behind
us on a cart. A whistling cannonball demolished the
ridge where Bad Jace had been sniping us, causing an
avalanche of debris to fall down the side of the outer
canyon wall.

"Wow," I said. "Snake, your girlfriend is a keeper."

Despite a painful wound, he chuckled. "Her Mormon
daddy cast that gun."

"To do what?"

"Defend plural marriage by killing US soldiers in Utah."

Three saloon ladies took turns blasting at the ridge with Winchester rifles. This gave Estrella moments to reload the Napoleon Cannon. She worm-swabbed the barrel with what looked like an old mop, extinguishing the hot embers before dropping in a gunpowder package. She rammed it to the back of the barrel with the other end of the mop. Then she tossed in a batch of grapes with more gunpowder, rammed it in, and shoved a piece of newspaper into the quill hole.

I said to Snake, "She's not really going to—"

Estrella struck a match off the cannon stock, lit the fuse, and yelled, "Hole!" The women stopped firing and sprinted away from the big gun.

"Oh my—" My words were cut off.

The blast devastated the boulders that had been bulwarking Bad Jace.

Things were quiet for a spell after that. The saloon ladies kept their rifles trained, but there was no response. I took a chance and, Sharps in hand, began climbing the ridge. When I reached the top, there was nothing there save for a couple of shells and Bad Jace's heavy footprints. I peered down into the canyon and saw nothing. He'd stolen away on his horse, heading toward, I assumed, the real hydrogen wagon, where he was storing it.

"He's gone!" I yelled to everyone.

The saloon ladies cheered, pumping their rifles in the air with both hands. It crossed my mind that I could do worse than hire these maneaters to help me safeguard the President. But they were distractingly pretty, and Poppy wouldn't approve. Plus, I didn't know them from

Eve. They might have been wilder and less disciplined than Snake.

I stepped carefully down the ridge to consult with Estrella, already inspecting Snake's neck gash. He was sitting on the ground next to the wagon. The bandage I'd improvised was holding.

"You'll live," she said. "Tincture?"

Snake nodded, refusing to look at her.

She brought out a bottle of laudanum. When Snake opened his mouth, she pinched the rubber eye dropper bulb to feed him some relief mama-bird style.

"You're a heavy gunner and a medic," I said.

She smiled. "I'm a woman in the wilderness."

"Any idea where Bad Jace is hiding the wagon?"

"I'd say in another part of Rhyolite Cave. There's a trail that leads out of that canyon."

"My tracking skills are shaky," I said.

"Your horse is solid, though." Indeed, my sorrel was standing a dozen yards from us, still chewing the same patch of burro-weed.

"Estrella—"

"You want us to clean all this up so you can track and kill Bad Jace."

"I'm on a job, and your help is appreciated." I reached into my coat for greenbacks to give to her.

"I'm not accepting currency at this moment. Bad Jace has caused too much commotion for the good women of Rattlepeak. He requires killing for having disturbed our beauty sleep."

"After I snuff him, you'll be compensated for your efforts here."

"Don't let her fool you, Tiny," Snake interrupted. "Estrella doesn't require compensation. She creates mayhem for the sheer pleasure."

"I'll make you walk back if you don't pipe down."

"Don't worry, darling," he said. "I can still brush your hair with my good arm."

"Can you lend me a rifle?" I said. "Shooting a Sharps on horseback will send me flying."

Estrella threw a look at the prettiest saloon lady.

The blue-eyed woman tossed me her Winchester, which I succeeded in catching and propping on my shoulder. She flounced her way over to me, removed her bonnet, and planted a kiss as cool as an oasis on my chapped lips. Her breath was like a high-desert apricot sweetened by the sun.

Then she took off her bandolier loaded with bullets and handed it to me like an article of lingerie.

"I think the heat," I said, wiping my forehead with my coat sleeve, "is getting to me."

"The saloon ladies of Rattlepeak have that effect on men," Estrella said.

I retrieved my grapple-bow and shoved it and the borrowed Winchester into the same scabbard. Moments later, I was charging my sorrel into the canyon through which Bad Jace had retreated and escaped. My mount was tired, but I expected Bad Jace's was too. I hated pushing my horse so hard, especially on the messy terrain of a wash. But if I didn't reach Bad Jace in time, he'd be off with the wagon for which I'd been hired to ferry back to Virginia City. Grinaker's money was good, but I had to clear Chaparral's debts and recover his Mormon girlfriend's peepstone.

The other idea haunting me was that Grinaker might want the wagon for nefarious purposes. If so, there was a chance I could get the Confederate sympathizer to reveal his intent.

Or the machinations of other unsavory types.

When I emerged from the canyon, Bad Jace's tracks led me into a landscape of red sandstone and desert pines. A caravan had come through here not long ago, with stumps of trees looking freshly axe-hewn and a few shattered wagon frames sitting in waist-high stretches of buffalograss. When the trail began to rise up onto a bluff against a lush horizon, I brought my sorrel to a stop, listening to the silent and lovely expanse, and sniffing the air for my gruesome quarry.

My horse whinnied, which alerted me that someone was approaching. I dismounted, tethered my beast, and easily climbed one of the pines, standing on a lower limb. Through the branches of needles, I could see a hundred yards in any direction, and over the hill. I heard voices speaking to one another, and then I saw three riders coming straight down the sloped path, heading right for me. I could tell that they were road agents, highway robbers searching for a soft mark.

Worried about being pressed from behind, I checked to confirm Bad Jace wasn't sneaking up. Satisfied, I climbed down and positioned my horse behind some pines. I waited, kneeling on one knee, Winchester resting across my thigh as the riders came down the path. They hadn't noticed my presence, so I waited for one of them to start talking again before I announced myself.

"If you have peaceful intentions," I said sternly, "keep on in this direction. If your business is thieving, however, you'd best turn around and take another route."

"We're on our way into the canyon," the leader said. "We're camping there for the evening. See, we plan to build a church in Rattlepeak."

"I've met the good people of Rattlepeak. They don't need a church. They want nothing save more outlaws to hang. I've met plenty of carpenters too. You don't have their appearance."

The trio of bandits didn't respond. I could see them scanning the pines, trying to determine where I was positioned, trying to pinpoint the location of my voice. Then the leader said, still playing his role, "That's not what we heard. It's all womenfolk running the town. They require men with strong backs to, *ahem*, erect a structure for them to enjoy. Words of God and such."

"I am the word of God for you in this moment," I said, stepping out now into the path, rifle aimed at the leader. "And I'm telling you, sinners, you must turn back now. There's no chance in hell that you'll set foot in that canyon. Except perhaps in a coffin, which is also, I'll add, the only chance any of you three will ever have of ending up in a church."

"Adolescent boy," another bandit said gruffly to his leader. "Scrawny trifle. Gun him down."

"If this here is the only obstacle between me and unlimited girl parts, I say we cut him down," the third fool agreed.

Part of me wanted to subject them to the untender mercies of Estrella and her saloon ladies. But I didn't want to put them out any more than I already had.

I knew the leader would start talking just before he slapped leather. He looked like the type.

"See here, son—" And he drew iron.

I smashed a bullet into his skull, splitting it like an overripe melon.

I'd lever-actioned another round when the other two, obviously experienced killers, sideways crab-walked to avoid my next shot. They raised their pistols, and it was on.

I wrecked the faster one's tibia with a blast, his body crumpling like scythed wheat in a field. His screams were so loud they seemed to vibrate my hat as I pulled my Colt revolver and got off a shot that nearly ripped the third bandit's left arm from his body.

He managed to get off a round that I thought momentarily tagged me, but he'd struck the chinstrap on my gaucho hat, missing flesh and bone.

The two of them writhed on the ground in blood-soaked agony, unable to raise their pistols or to even focus on my advancing presence. When I reached the bandit with the severed arm, I shot him point-blank. When I stood over the one with the bone-snapped leg, I blasted his gun mitt into pulp. Then I pressed my boot into his chest as he shrieked, pinning him like a butterfly.

"Stop that noise," I said.

He sobbed, gasped. "You, you—"

"You saw a man on the trail. Tell me about him."

"Wounded. Says he..." He screamed again.

Aware of the monster inside tentacling its way into my mind, I stepped harder, my boot heel stomping his collarbone. "What did he say?"

"He has a wagon full of hydrogen. Stuff that makes balloons float."

"Where is he?"

"You're the Kid, ain't you," he said, the corners of his mouth cracking from blood loss. "I—I see it now. You're Kid Crimson."

"Last time. Where is he."

"Stoner and the rest are heading to the caves in Rhyolite."

"Stoner *Kurgin*?"

He nodded vigorously, desperately. "Hey, I need a doctor. Stoner has a medicine bag. We can save my leg. I just need to pull the metal—"

"No one is saved," I said, my voice no longer my own. I shot him again, sparing him further pain.

11

Rhyolite Cave sat abandoned when I arrived, convincing me I'd beaten Stoner Kurgin to the punch. On instinct, I took a chance navigating a narrow cliff path that most riders wouldn't risk. It was steep and scary in places, but it led directly to the caverns. At the biggest cave, there was no sign of a disturbance or struggle, no sounds. Had the bandits really captured the formidable Bad Jace? Maybe the dead man I'd killed had uttered something ridiculous to throw me off the scent of his companions.

I obscured my horse a half mile from the caverns, then took up a position behind an elevated rock formation. Using a pair of field glasses, I watched everything, hoping to catch a glimpse of someone moving in and around the mouth of the biggest cave.

It wasn't long before my patience was rewarded. I saw the creature known as Stoner and another rider unhorse. The sight of these two outlaws made my blood boil. They lit a lantern and made their way toward the darkness. I recognized them from a tense encounter we'd shared in

Silver Reef, Utah, years earlier. A water rights dispute that went sideways. I ended up having to clobber men on both sides of the conflict. The side that had originally hired me brought in Stoner to escalate the ordeal into straight-up murder of the opposing camp, which I refused. Fortunately, for everyone involved, I'd viciously neutralized the whole dustup by the time Stoner and his partner arrived. I met them briefly in the town saloon, exchanging menacing glares. Since he hadn't been wired an advance and had no retainer, there was nothing at stake for him. I finished my whiskey and returned to Virginia City.

This time, however, a confrontation was unavoidable.

Stoner and his pal went into the cave. Minutes later, they came out to fetch their horses and bring them inside to pull the wagon out into the light. I had my Winchester ready, but I didn't want to take them out until I knew for certain the location of the wagon and Bad Jace. Killing a couple of clueless if deserving idiots without confirmation wasn't my style.

The horses emerged, followed by the stagecoach, Stoner and his friend in the driver's box. They were calm, leisurely, giving the impression that they didn't feel pressured or pursued. I had the wagon in sight, but the secondary part of my mission—figuring out Bad Jace's angle—was fuzzy. I needed to secure the missing piece of this puzzle.

They settled into the trail that led to Rattlepeak, which gave me more reason to observe them from a distance first, and then shoot them down like miserable wretches later. I hustled back to saddle up my sorrel, careful not to make noise. I stayed far enough behind them I could make out the shape of the wagon from half a mile away, losing them for a moment whenever there was a bend or bank in the path. They continued on, never stopping or meeting anyone along the way, to a desert whiskey stop, where Snake was, in my mind's eye, lying in bed, recovering from a bullet wound, surrounded by lovely, armed-to-the-teeth saloon ladies and a cannonball-blasting brothel madam.

I'd only lived a few years in Nevada, but I felt I could say with total confidence that the Silver State was a realm of unbridled yet endearing insanity. It was a place of giddy depravity, and I was sure I'd miss it when I left to become a fruit farmer in California.

Through my field glasses, I watched the wagon halt in front of Estrella's establishment. The two men got out and walked into the saloon, leaving their cargo unguarded. I counted three horses tethered to the hitching post. Estrella kept her animals penned in the corral behind the main structure, so that meant that there were at least five men inside the bar at the moment.

I cantered up to the water well to give my horse a drink, then tied him up so I could move silently and investigate. There was no more dead Dobie littering the grounds, no more buzzing flies. The smell of cooked meat was in the air, and I heard raucous laughter from inside, a friendly poker game underway or a conversation punctuated with a ribald joke.

When I stepped up to the porch, I heard Estrella's voice. She didn't sound stressed or besieged. She was talking to the men, not flirtatiously, but with the stubborn generosity of a bar manager looking to part her customers from their money by any means necessary. Figuring none of the men inside knew I was in town or why I was here, I pushed my way through the batwing doors.

The silence was impressive. Stoner Kurgin and three men were lined up along the bar. I didn't see the fifth, which bothered me. But then perhaps the horse was Bad Jace's, stolen by these miscreants.

Pouring a shot of whiskey for Stoner, Estrella was the last to look up at me, giving me a wink.

"Kid," she said. "It's been too long. Have a seat."

For a moment, I thought she had suddenly thrown in with Stoner and his hydrogen wagon-boosting gang. Anything was possible in a town like Rattlepeak. But there was something in her voice that clearly communicated to me that she was playing a role for our temporary benefit.

Best to play along.

"I'll have a shot of your rotgut, Estrella," I said. "Seen my colleague?"

Stoner stayed silent, his men drinking their whiskey. It was obvious from his expression he recognized me from Silver Creek. The scowl he shot me was dagger-sharp.

"Who might your friend be, Kid?" she said delightfully, pouring me a shot that we both knew I wouldn't have a chance to drink.

"Fellow who goes by the name Bad Jace."

Everyone's face at the bar dropped. Stoner had had enough. He slammed down his glass, pricked up, and pointed his finger at me. "This is the second time you've put your nose in my business. It's the last time. Boy, before I gun you down in the street, what's your interest in Bad Jace."

"Yeah, how do you know him, punk?" snarled his shorter buddy, the one with him on the wagon. He had a huge knife scar on his face that I imagined myself improving with my fist. "You a friend of his? Or are you a bounty hunter looking to collect."

From behind the bar, Estrella smiled at me and nodded, letting me know she had my back. As she reached for a rifle, she studied the four men who were gathering close and walking toward me as if ready to rush.

The monster inside me began to unlock its flimsy shackles.

I said nothing more, heightening their agitation.

"I don't like how you mince, molly-houser," the scarred one said. "I could fix that right quick."

"Freakshow," I growled in a voice not quite my own. "You're the one getting redesigned."

He swung and barely clipped my chin. He didn't have solid footing, the impact minuscule.

I unbuckled my gun and feinted a handoff to Stoner, suggesting I intended to conduct a pure brawl. Confused, he reached out to receive it.

Then I withdrew it and savagely backhand-whipped the belt, mostly the holstered iron, across the bridge of the scarfaced bandit's nose, breaking it.

Blood-masked, he fell back against a saloon table, shattering it.

Stoner went to grab me. I whipped my Colt from its holster and shot off the front of one of his boots, amputating his toes. He fell over, writhing.

The other two bandits charged me. The closer one threw what he intended to be a haymaker, but I ducked under it. I put my shoulder down and rammed him in the stomach. He went flying, spine cracking noisily against the bar. Grinning, Estrella rifle-butted him into a sudden nap.

The last bandit tried to wrench the pistol from my

gun hand, but I'd seen him coming. I pivot-rolled in the direction he was pulling, allowing him to get his fingers around the gun with the barrel pointed away from us. The moment he thought he had control of the weapon I twisted the barrel toward his chest as his index finger caught and snapped completely off inside the trigger guard. The Colt discharged, blasting a hole through his chest and splattering blood. He crumpled in a gory heap, relinquishing my gun to me like a scarecrow with its stuffing yanked out.

"Boss," said Scarface through a mouthful of blood, face oozing as he lay in a heap of table fragments. "I think the boy ain't what he seems… I think he's—"

"Kid Crimson," Estrella said, smirking, rifle on her shoulder. "You boys are screwed."

I reached for blood-burbling Scarface, pulled him to his boots, held him by his vest lapels, and brutally head-butted his already-mulched beak. Knocked unconscious, he fell backward onto his deceased buddy with a hole blown through his chest.

Stoner was crawling on his elbows toward the saloon exit, a sanguinary streak in his wake.

I caught up with him, pressed my boot against his shattered foot, and twisted my heel.

He screamed something fierce.

"Where's Bad Jace, Stoner," I said.

Stoner couldn't answer given how much pain I was inflicting on him. And I knew it. He sobbed and pleaded for mercy, but the monster was out now. It would take a moment to tamp him down.

Suddenly, the atmosphere in the room changed. There was a foul, brackish odor. I sensed the presence of the very animal I was seeking.

Gun holstered, Bad Jace stood at the threshold,

pressing a hand to a bloody arm. He'd been wounded in a skirmish with, I assumed, the men I had just dismantled. His boots were dusty, having walked a great distance to get here. His was the fifth horse outside the saloon. Stoner's gang likely planned to sell or trade it.

"Kid," Bad Jace said, voice hoarse. "Looks like you did me a favor."

I removed my boot from Stoner's destroyed foot and raised my Colt toward Bad Jace. "And you've done me none. Tell me why shouldn't I kill you right now for shooting my friend?"

Bad Jace limped over to an empty table and gingerly took a seat. "I didn't shoot him, Kid. Stoner there, the whimpering man whose foot you shot off, is the one that done shot your friend. You know his reputation as a sniper."

The part about Stoner being a distance gunner in the Mexican American War was checked out. "What about Dobie?"

"Dobie changed the location for the deal," Bad Jace said, "because of all the pressure bearing down on him. He moved the wagon here to Rattlepeak after some Union boys got word of what he planned to bring through Fort Baker and into Lone Pine."

"Didn't work. Bluebellies ended up here anyway."

Bad Jace nodded. "Deserters with sensitive intel. Dobie pretended to lose a poker bet after fashioning a dummy wagon so that I could take them out. Still, they caused problems."

"I'll say. Dobie's dead."

"You took care of them when I couldn't. I knew the shoeshine boy would pass along the message that the deal had changed."

He'd figured out about Ezra. Not good. "You're

telling me, with a straight face, that Stoner caught you as you were chasing the Union boys."

"That's what I'm saying."

"I scented you out there," I said, "before the Sharps started firing."

Bad Jace shrugged, wincing from the pain of moving his shoulders. "I'm telling the truth."

"Estrella, tell me your opinion," I said to the woman, still holding a rifle in her hands.

She was silent for a beat. Then she said, "I don't exactly know what sounds correct. But let me warn you now, Kid. My dearest friend in the world, my handsome Snake, is upstairs in this establishment. He's recovering from being bullet-gouged in the neck. And if I ever see you or this pungent mockery of a man show up to my saloon again, I will shoot you both dead."

"Understood, ma'am," Bad Jace whispered, looking shaky, in need of medical attention.

Then Estrella came around from the bar with the rifle, stood over the groaning Stoner Kurgin, and put a bullet in the back of his head. He didn't make another sound after that.

She walked to the customer side of the bar and pounded the whiskey shot she had poured for me. A few of her ladies brought out a bucket of hot water, a bottle of white vinegar, and a mop.

Estrella poured herself another shot and gave me a hard look. "Your turn to clean, pretty boy."

Bad Jace fell out of his chair and onto the saloon floor.

12

Thickly bandaged and heavily medicated from the whiskey Estrella and her saloon ladies kept pouring into him, Snake embraced me rather dramatically in front of the wagon. Instead of an empty crate placed on the thoroughbrace of the stagecoach we had chased across the desert, the real wagon's hydrogen container was built directly into the chassis.

"Sure there's hydrogen in this contraption?" I said.

Bad Jace approached, himself wearing a sling and looking alcohol-numbed. He used his good arm to unfasten a hose with a nozzle from the carriage. He pulled a lever on the vehicle that generated a hissing sound. He pulled a stormproof match from his vest pocket, scratched it against the wagon, and placed it in front of the gas emanating from the nozzle.

Suddenly, a massive torrent of flame erupted, startling Snake enough he gasped aloud and nearly singeing my eyebrows.

"I'd wager," Bad Jace said, shutting off the valve and

extinguishing the fire much to everyone's relief, "that this here wagon is filled to the brim."

"Why did the Rebs waste hydrogen on air balloons," Snake asked, "when they can barbecue the entire Union army with one of these?"

"Because when this machine is hit with a cannonball," Bad Jace explained, "it's like a bomb going off inside your lines. And they make easy-to-spot targets for bluebellied snipers."

"Good to know that we're traveling on an explosive wagon," I said. "Let's move."

My Paiute friend gave me yet another hug, waiting for Bad Jace as he struggled to step up into the wagon. Then Snake whispered to me, "Brother, I'll miss you. Watch out for this demon. He can't be trusted. He leaks dark magic wherever he roams."

"I'm aware. There's a chance I'll need his gunmanship to return safely to Virginia City. Word has gotten out about the wagon."

"Hope he's right-handed," Snake said. "His left arm doesn't look good."

"He is," I said. "Focus on getting healthy. Too much drinking will slow your recovery."

He nodded. "Sorry about Estrella. She means well, she's just— well, she's just so damn sassy!"

"Estrella is wonderful. Marry her soon."

"I intend to."

"Take care of my sorrel."

"I will. You know I love horses."

"See you, Snake."

"Until next time, Tiny."

I pulled myself up into the driver's seat and grabbed the reins. On my right, I had my Sharps and grapple-bow, unscabbarded and at the ready. On my left, Bad Jace fought to get comfortable with his tender wing. He smelled better. When he'd passed out, I paid the ladies that worked in Estrella's saloon to strip and scrub him like a sedated ox using carbolic soap flakes and long-handled bath brushes. They burned his clothes and outfitted Bad Jace with a huge shirt and black denim from a box of clothes that a storekeeper had left behind after a drinking binge en route to Utah.

"How many bandits are gunning for us?" I said.

"Bandits, Paiutes, Utes, Union deserters, Mormons," Bad Jace said. "The whole world seeks to nab this wagon now that the fools at Fort Baker heard about it."

"Well, get your gun arm ready."

He grunted, affirming he was prepared to inflict damage. His Winchester rifle with the brass scope lay across his lap, barrel pointed away from me. I didn't trust him entirely, even if he knew he needed me to get back to Virginia City in one piece. I wanted to finish this job and hold sweet Poppy in my arms again before the President of what was left of the United States arrived to tour the silver mines and visit the ostentatious homes of Nevada's *nouveau riche*.

Time to get home. I said nothing to Bad Jace. Instead, I snapped the reins on the horse team. We wheeled away from Rattlepeak and into the sprawling Nevada desert.

We rode for several hours. The trail we followed was hard-beaten by the weight of thousands of wagons burdened with silver ore and forlorn, toothless miners stricken with a get-rich-quick dream. We didn't speak to each other for much of that first day's ride, Bad Jace chewing the most horrid smelling tobacco I'd ever had the umbrage of hearing someone chew. From his wagon seat, he spat huge globs of chaw juice into the dust, every now and then rolling his shoulder. He was smarter than I realized. By keeping his arm moving rather than letting it stiffen and lose blood flow, he was healing faster than he would've otherwise. It was something my father had instilled in me at an early age. When badly injured, you had to move, even with the worst kind of pain. It was a useful lesson, literally and metaphorically. It was why, after nearly getting my neck stretched for falling in love with an enslaved woman on my father's plantation, I had to escape Georgia. I could've easily killed dozens, even a hundred, lunatic racists in the South. I could've made revenge my life's mission. But there was no chance I'd have successfully killed *all* of the lunatics. I moved to stay alive, to heal my wounds, and to build a new identity. However, Virginia City was often acutely similar to the South. Men like Bad Jace cropped up everywhere in Nevada. They weren't as virulent as the murderers who butchered my beloved. Yet the Nevada strain of villainy was ferociously heartless.

I was reminded of this when I watched Bad Jace pick up his rifle and, with one good arm, shoot a coyote that had been running alongside us for a while, hoping for a scrap of something to eat.

The animal yelped, writhed, then fell still. Bad Jace chuckled at his own senseless cruelty.

"Save your bullets, Bad Jace."

"I always have lead for a coyote."

"Why?"

He shrugged. "They're scavengers. They got it coming. Vultures, too."

"Scavengers are necessary. They clean the land."

"And then I clean the land of them."

"Be merciful, as your God is merciful," I said.

"Bible?"

"You know about it. Imagine my shock."

"I know a lot of things that would shock you."

I turned to give him a hooded stare. "Doubtful."

We rode in silence for a long time after that, keeping a watchful eye on a darkening bank of bruise-colored clouds. The tips of the cottonwoods began waving; leaves on the aspens twinkling. Soon a low roar was audible, and the rising wind came in gusts, with intervals of cool, light breezes. Gradually, there was a steady gust and sudden whirling currents. The clouds began to loosen, stretching and spreading over the valley, rolling quickly.

Bad Jace fastened his coat and pulled his hat tightly around his skull. "We don't need this."

"We need shelter," I said.

"See that canyon? There's a nest of sandstone we can wedge ourselves against."

"I was thinking that."

I slapped the reins as a gale swooped down with a hollow, unearthly howl.

THE SUN FINISHED its descent and twilight faded into darkness as we reached the sandstone. Careful not to damage our wheel, I carefully squeezed the wagon deep inside a craggy rock cluster that shielded us from buffeting gusts. Steadily the wind increased its strength, making hideous noises as it unleashed its power.

I released the horses, but they refused to budge from the minimal shelter. I re-harnessed them and threw heavy blankets over each of their heads to dampen the mayhem. Gritty particles stinging us like flying needles, Bad Jace and I crawled across the cargo area and sand-wiched ourselves underneath the baggage storage frame, which was chained to the chassis. The noise was so loud it seemed God was sculpting the geologies around us. When He was done with the rocks, He'd grind us into pleasing shapes too.

Black night and roaring wind engulfed us. I couldn't see my companion, even though we found ourselves pressed together. I suffered the torture of his fetid breath and his miserable growling. I couldn't get the baggage door to close sufficiently enough to keep airborne sand from lacerating us. I decided to check the cable chain for snags. Handkerchief covering my nose and mouth, I climbed atop the cargo area again. Suddenly, the sky cracked open. A blue-white, dazzling streak of lightning illuminated the desert, every rock and cactus luminously bright, vivid.

The lightning also spotlit three figures with bandannas covering their faces, wind nearly pushing them to the ground, trudging toward us with knives brandished.

I'd never fought for my life outnumbered during an evening windstorm alongside a stone killer with only one good arm.

Chaparral was making me earn every cent of my debt forgiveness plan.

I leaned down into the baggage storage to scream, "Grab a knife! Bastards have arrived!"

I jumped off the wagon and was immediately wind-blown. My shoulder smashed an unlit lamp adjacent to the driver's box, shards of glass slicing me. Bleeding before the fighting started, I didn't lose my balance on the silt and gravel, which saved my life.

I had my Bowie ready for the first assailant with only desert moonlight to go by. His plodding approach made him appear like an ancient spirit materializing from another dimension to stalk me underwater. He lunged. I parried downward, then slashed upward. I messed up, lodging my knife under his jaw, unable to pull it out. Trying to rip my Bowie loose, I unintentionally drew him closer. Even as he died, I'd given him a chance to stab my outer forearm. Not a serious wound, but it hurt like the devil. I screamed, but in the din of a dust storm there was hardly a sound.

Then was another flash of lightning and deafening thunder. The two other attackers revealed themselves within striking distance. No weapon to rely on, I retreated without turning my back to them. I tripped over a wagon wheel. The Paiute closer to me raised his blade, eyes aglint.

The assassin's hand disappeared in a flash of gunfire, a point-blank blast from Bad Jace's rifle. The bandanna fell from the Paiute's face as he opened his mouth to scream and dropped to his knees in agony. Hot blood geysered from the stump, splashing me. I got to my feet with a rock in my hand and bashed his forehead, breaking it open.

At that moment, the third assassin threw an axe at Bad Jace. He'd been smart enough to hold his rifle sideways. The Paiute's weapon somehow sliced through the wind and struck the gun with enough force that the Winchester broke in half. Another huge gust caught Bad Jace, and he tumbled off the wagon and onto the ground in front me.

I launched myself to tackle the last of the killers, but I ended up tripping over Bad Jace, The Paiute had me prone, his granite fingers on my neck, choking me. He tried to gouge my eyeballs into my brain, so I bit his palm, tasting his blood. The gore mixed with the sand in my mouth created a horrifying sludge. He finally let go, and I sprung at him, convinced I shouldn't give him a moment to get his balance.

Another lightning flash. In that second, I saw the Paiute's face pulverized by the iron anchor hurtling from my grapple-bow. I looked behind me and saw Bad Jace holding it, standing there, moon-beamed and storm-blasted, like a specter from Dante's second circle of Hell. I couldn't see his face, but I could tell from his posture that he was bone-weary.

We said nothing, both of us exhausted from battle and the skin-shredding storm. The inventory of damage was significant: A gash in my forearm. Bad Jace's good shoulder was now bad from his fall. I was having some trouble breathing from my near strangulation and the taste of blood lingering on my palate.

We stomped headlong against the gale and climbed slowly into the storage area of the hydrogen wagon and slept, hoping that the tumult might soon pass.

13

"WELL, I'VE HAD WORSE NIGHTMARES." BAD Jace yawned with a bear-like snarl, dust falling from his shaggy mane. He attempted to stretch his massive arms to the dawn, but the pain from his injuries made him yelp in agony.

I unhooked the baggage storage chain. The sun was temperate, brilliant, not a cloud in the sky. The wind had ceased; the air was cool. Anxious to eat something, the horses pawed at the ground, vocalizing their hunger.

"I haven't," I said to Bad Jace. My arm had stopped bleeding but there was a stinging, burning sensation. The cut on my shoulder throbbed. A shot of liquor would've patched me up fine.

I walked to the front of the wagon and reached under the driver's box for a sack of hay and a canteen that I'd packed for the trip. After I fed and watered the animals, I lit the kindling and put on the coffee. Then I took a moment to investigate our dead assailants.

Buried under the sand, they looked like skeletons left to bleach in the desert. I grabbed each one by the hair to inspect their faces. I didn't recognize any of them, but I was certain that they were Paiutes, though from what tribe I couldn't determine. Hopefully not Snake's.

Bad Jace coughed up phlegm and spat into fire. Without saying a word, we removed our boots, shaking the dust out of them. We turned our pockets inside out and snapped our coats until they were reasonably free of silt and pebbles. I swished water from the same canteen I'd used to hydrate the horses, clearing my teeth of grit and Paiute blood.

Turkey buzzards were circling by the time we finished our coffee. I scoured the perimeter for the bag of biscuits Snake had given me, but there was no trace. We'd have to ride out on empty stomach, unsettled by harsh black coffee and memories of last night's brutality. It took nearly an hour to push the excess sand from the wagon and to disentangle the team's harness. Eventually, we started rolling down the trail again.

I practiced in my mind before uttering the words aloud: "I appreciate you saving me from getting hatcheted last night."

Bad Jace grunted. "You saw them coming at us in the dark."

"The lightning spared us, I guess."

"Let me take back that lie I spoke."

"Which one?"

"I've never had a nightmare worse than that."

I nodded.

We agreed to abandon the trail to avoid another attack. Bad Jace knew of a forgotten Mormon path that ran east of Ash Creek beyond a series of limestone caverns. It took us nearly all day, and we saw what might've been bandits a few miles in the distance. With my Sharps, I felt invincible during the daylight. Night-time was another matter.

When we reached the caves, I hopped off the wagon and used a salt desert shrub to cover our tracks for a good hundred yards. Then I jumped back on and picked up my field glasses, scanning the horizon.

"I see a village."

"Chief Tutsagavit," Bad Jace said. "He's been out here for years. The missionaries softened him up with their lamb-lies-down-with-the-lion preaching. They left when the war started."

"Will the chief give us food for one of our horses?"

"We won't need to swap a horse."

"We've nothing to trade."

"Whiskey."

I couldn't believe what I heard. "You stole from Estrella."

"I'll pay her back."

"With your blood. It's funny, because I was thinking a drink might put me on solid footing."

"You worry too much, Kid." He pulled the bottle from his sheepskin coat. "Nip?"

"Stating a fact is all," I said, waving away the hooch. "I hope your chief is thirsty for liquor, because I'm famished."

"Tutsagavit doesn't drink."

"You think a teetotaler will feed us if we give him whiskey?"

"His wives," Bad Jace assured. "They need strong liquor."

I couldn't argue with that. After all, my own mother drank everything she could find in Georgia to cushion herself from my father's vicious abuse.

We reached the wickiups and were received warmly

by the people. Though there were a few events taking place that raised Bad Jace's hackles and aroused my suspicion. The first was an exorcism that an old spell-binder was performing on a sick woman. It was a quiet ceremony, but when the subject began to convulse and twitch, Bad Jace's ugly visage began to show disgust, fear even. While that was occurring, a gloomy funeral was underway near the center of the village. The air was filled with the sound of drums, flutes, and rattles made from animal bones.

"Savages," Bad Jace growled under his breath.

"If you insult these beautiful people," I said, "before I've had a chance to eat, I'll gut you."

He harrumphed, bringing the cart up to the chief's brushwood hut.

The chief didn't greet us. Instead, we were met by a young woman in a grass skirt and a rabbit-skin shirt. Her expression was stoic, especially given the news she conveyed. She was, as I had described the tribe before laying eyes on her, gorgeous.

"Chief Tutsagavit has fallen ill, and might be dying," she said. "He insists that you stay for supper and camp here for the night."

The sun was setting as we stepped off the wagon. Bad Jace removed his hat before presenting her with the whiskey. He was speechless in the presence of the chief's lovely daughter. She didn't immediately accept the gift, however.

"Please tell Chief Tutsagavit we are grateful," I said. "What's your name?"

"Shell Flower," she said, locking eyes with me.

"That's my wife's name. Flower."

Bad Jace chuckled at my slight fibbing.

Shell Flower ignored him. "Where is your wife?"

"She's in Virginia City. She runs a business there."

Having absorbed this information, she took the whiskey from Bad Jace.

"Our evening meal is being prepared in the cooking pit next," she said. "Please help yourself." She turned around and headed back inside the chief's hut. Bad Jace and I looked at each other, and then my stomach growled audibly.

We went over to where the smoke was coming from. My companion wasn't impressed with the aroma, wrinkling his nose. Women were grinding seeds by the light of the moon and boiling pottage in a conical dish made from clay and sand. It was a darkish gray mess with bacon chunks in it. The women smiled at me and shared a comment that I didn't hear.

They stopped smiling when Bad Jace stepped into view.

I took the liberty of tasting the flour which the women were making from seeds of grass by rubbing them between two rocks. It tasted like buckwheat flour or bean meal. Then I discerned that what I had presumed to be bacon was, in fact, bunches of matted ants.

One of the women stirred the porridge with a ladle made from the horn of a mountain sheep. She divided the mess into wicker baskets, which were then distributed to the elder women gathered around the cooking pit. After the elders were served, the same woman encouraged us to sit on blankets by the fire. Then she brought porridge baskets along with a special plate stacked with a roasted porcupine, including brains and bone yet sans quills, plus several roasted sand larks.

"You're not really," Bad Jace said.

"So hungry right now," I said, "I could eat your boots."

"When you bleed internally, I'll provide a mercy bullet."

"They don't have barbs on the inside, you absolute cretin."

He slurped his gruel with a wince, then nearly heaved it back up.

I sucked the strangely seasoned meat from the bones of the porcupine. Then I crunched into and wolfed down the entirety of a lark—beak, feathers, feet.

The women smiled at my gustatory pleasure. They didn't know that I'd spent months eating exactly this kind of food with Snake as I healed from my injuries at Pyramid Lake.

I noticed a young girl, maybe ten years old wearing a ceremonial dress and headband. She looked adorable and wide-eyed, like Ezra the shoeshine boy. She ate impassively, though, without delight. She seemed resigned to a fate not of her choosing.

"Who's the girl?" I said to the serving woman. "She's too young to marry."

The woman replied, "She is the chief's Suffering Girl."

"I don't understand."

"Tutsagavit wants her sacrificed. So that his sickness will go away and then he will feel better."

I said nothing. My appetite faded.

Next to me, Bad Jace slurped and heaved again before bumping me with his elbow.

"Told you, Kid," he said, tossing his basket of mush at the dirt. "Savages."

———

THEY BEGAN SLAUGHTERING horses at midnight, twenty shot dead in the span of a few minutes. It was terrifying to witness. Even Bad Jace, the coyote-slayer, looked visibly disturbed by the noise of so many animals dying in such cruel fashion. Despite hosting missionaries for several years, despite being bombarded with the message of Christian love and compassion, the tribe was under the sway of a chief who'd lost his mind from severe illness. I wasn't permitted to diagnose him or pay him a visit. If I had, there was no medicine for me to dispense. I had quinine on me for malaria, but such a disease was rare in this part of Nevada.

Having fed us, the tribe became disinterested, as if their responsibility to us was done. They focused now on meeting Tutsagavit's horrible demands. He apparently believed that killing a herd of horses, as well as the village's prettiest Paiute child, would alleviate his misery. He was, in other words, insane and willing to hurt children to feel better about his miserable life.

Just like my father.

Bad Jace didn't require much convincing. He readied the horses and prepped our wagon for a fast getaway while I searched for the girl. After supper, she'd been taken from the vicinity of the cooking pit and sequestered somewhere near the chief's hut. Fortunately, I encountered Shell Flower, who presumed I was in need of tobacco. Drunk from the whiskey Bad Jace gave her, she furnished me a pipe. In the process of securing it, she pulled back a tent flap to reveal the girl's small body trussed to an old, rusted, iron carriage shaft likely brought here by missionaries.

I thanked Shell Flower, said goodnight, and sauntered in the direction of my wagon, only to double back after a minute. At the tent, I saw no one standing guard. I quickly went inside with my Bowie knife glinting. When I locked eyes with the tied-up girl in her sacrificial garb, she looked primed to scream. But I comically shoved my knife into its sheath, pretending to fumble it a bit as one might entertain a dimwitted child. Her expression switched to one of intrigue.

"You're not a man of God," she said softly and with a measure of concern.

"I think I am, though, for you," I said, "at least in this moment. My name is Crimson."

"Are you kidnapping me, Crimson Boy? Chief Tutsagavit needs me as a sacrifice so that his pain goes away. If he doesn't feel better, he may die."

"No kidnapping. Everyone dies, but it's not your time. What's your name?"

"Sarah."

"Sarah, I want you to be quiet and come with me."

"Where are we going?"

"To find the chief a better medicine woman," I lied, preparing to cut her straps away. "The one he has with him here is... well, she's inadequate to the task, let's just say."

"Chief Tutsagavit killed her a few minutes ago. Along with the horses."

"See? Exactly my point." I placed an index finger against my lips and whispered: "Let's go."

Before I could slice her binds, she stood up, straps falling away.

She rubbed her wrists, sensation returning. She had a small knife in her hand. She'd had it all along, hidden from Shell Flower and the rest. "I don't think you know any medicine women. But I will run faster than the wind with you, because I am suspicious of Chief Tutsagavit's spirit. A shadow lies upon it."

"That explains the blade."

She nodded.

"Wait, did I interrupt your escape attempt, Sarah?"

She nodded again, this time with a huge smile.

"I think you and I are going to get along really well."

"Yes. Now lead the way, Crimson Boy. I don't like it here anymore."

14

WE RODE THROUGH THE NIGHT AND KEPT A brisk pace through the Mojave. Every so often, Sarah woke from a nap and looked back, craning her neck over the cargo area to see if were being followed. She seemed disappointed that Chief Tutsagavit hadn't dispatched a wave of warriors.

"No one's coming," she said, arms crossed.

"Don't let it bother you," I said.

"Did they find another girl to sacrifice?"

"Possibly."

"Should we go back and rescue her?"

I shook my head. "We can't save everyone, Sarah. You're the one they intended to kill. Maybe the dead horses and medicine woman were enough to make him feel better."

She wrapped her arms around her stomach. "I'm hungry."

I pulled a roasted sand lark from my coat that I'd stowed during dinner and handed it to her. She gnawed on it greedily. She reminded me of the pugilists that I grew up with on the child-boxing circuit in the South. We were spunky oddballs, with no clue how to process the trauma that we were experiencing. We punched and hurt each other not to win bouts, but to impress one another, especially the older kids. The pecking order made everything strange, distancing, dreamlike. We never took the beatings we endured and inflicted personally. But we most certainly yearned to smash the authority figures who'd placed us in a revolting predicament.

I'd wanted to strike my father from a very young age. But when he hung my lover from an oak tree outside Macon, I knew at sixteen I had to try to kill him to keep him from killing me like he did my mother; to keep him from hurting others. My problem, naturally, was in the end, I was too similar to my father. We shared a propensity toward violence. Like corrupt father, like battered son. Adam had raised a Cain, because my father had allowed himself to be corrupted, to be contaminated by violence, a lust for power. He coped with his insanity by intentionally damaging me, trying to carve me into the most lethal version of himself, the Lucifer of Outer Georgia, invincible to all pain and a living weapon that no one could break. Ultimately, I was his victim, a sacrifice to his own unchecked ego.

Sarah was a victim of her tribal leader's madness, subjected to his ruthless whims. Where I was taking her, I had no idea. Probably Virginia City. It didn't matter so long as she kept moving, as *we* kept moving.

Sticking to Bad Jace's obscure Mormon trail still put us in contact with people. By late morning, we wheeled up to a copper deposit besieged by dozens of miners. A row of ragged cloth tents was lined up along the banks of a glittering arroyo. It eased my heart a little to see, in a landscape overrun with cholla cactus and yucca trees, water-loving cottonwood trees, their dangling leaves softly clattering in the wind. They offered bright promise in a barren world.

"It's beautiful here," Sara said.

"Yes," I said. "An oasis in the desert."

"Why are these men here?"

"They're here, because they want to transform the beauty of this place into money."

"Will it work?"

I nodded. "Unfortunately."

"I'll rest and water the horses," Bad Jace said, bringing our carriage to a stop. "You can drive us the rest of the way."

"Fine," I said, taking Sarah's hand as we stepped off. Soon we began making our way through a ramshackle mining town. Not that long ago Virginia City looked like this place.

The area was littered with old campfire sites full of rubbish and half-burnt logs, broken shovel shafts, and dented, rusted-through mining pans. Still, we enjoyed a marvelous view of the valley, a vast, treeless crust as parched as an elk hide, yet somehow contemplative and breathtaking. The sound of birds skittering across the creek's waterline for fish and flapping away was soothing.

There was a less pleasant noise emanating from deep within the assemblage of tents.

A group of miners was clustered around a covered wagon with a tall, expansive, white tarp. On its canvas, a giant disembodied arm with a bulging bicep was color-fully painted. Beneath the image blazed the words: DOKTOR SKORPION STRENGTH SERUM. A short, mustachioed man barkered in a thin, reedy voice from the rear of his wagon. He wore a striped top hat and a fancy striped suit accentuated his unserious, clownish demeanor. Everyone standing around him was transfixed, deeply considering whatever remedy he was pitching. I assumed it was a strength serum or muscle-growing snake oil because of the canvas rendering. As we stepped closer, I saw the salesman working the crowd masterfully.

There was a three-legged dog prancing wildly, if a bit oddly. Well, the number of legs could be debated. The animal had a fourth limb that was smaller and less functional than the rest. It hung limply near the spot where a normal dog limb should've appeared. The dog was a male, mixed breed—Basque shepherd, Border Collie—and was paying close attention to the salesman.

Sarah studied the animal and reached the same conclusion that I had.

She nudged me. "He was born with five legs."

"Yes," I said. "Looks like—"

"One of his good legs was amputated," she finished.

We stopped conversing so that we could hear what nonsense the salesman was slinging. Dr. Skorpion held a bottle, presenting it haughtily, like a sommelier, to his audience. He unleashed a torrent of rugged poetry full of innuendo and puffery.

"This here elixir puts the balls in your cannon, the powder in your musket, and the bullet in her chamber— if you understand what I'm saying now, my fellow gentle-misters and glorious doves of the morning!" He tipped his hat toward a tent of working girls who'd set up shop to service the miners. Situated adjacent to the audience, they laughed at Skorpion's elocution and flattery, scrubbing their laundry in basins of creek water heated over a fire.

"You'll dig twice as hard and find the motherlode before Monday," he went on. "All you need do is partake of a single swallow from a bottle of my proprietary blend of soothing herbs and healing Seneca oil, extracted from the rarest glands of the powerful croco-dragons in the mystical reaches of Bolivia, animals that live for five hundred years!"

"I hope your potion helps these boys *love* twice as hard," a dove heckled, slapping her thigh with the other cackling women.

"Love *me* like a croco-dragon, my big ol' miner of a man!" another mock-pleaded, clasping her hands together theatrically.

Skorpion seemed annoyed for a moment before a miner in the crowd yelled, "Huzzah! I'll take two bottles!" He proffered a handful of coins, which the salesman swapped for a bottle of his strength serum. The miner immediately uncorked it and to a slug, after which he emitted a wild hoot and went in the direction, presumably, of the claim he was working.

At this moment, the dog, on his three functioning legs, began to dazzle the audience. A furious yapper and a dedicated tail-wagger, he made his way toward the salesman. He picked up another bottle, poured some tincture into a tin cup, and placed it on the ground for the dog to drink.

After a few laps of the stuff, he barked proudly, then performed a backflip.

"It's a miracle," the salesman hollered, raising his arms to the sky with a huge grin.

More laughter and more sales as miners hurried to join the queue, bumping into one another and even swapping a few irritated shoves. Deprived of entertainment and stimulation in the desert wilderness, they were eager to give their money to a verbally gifted charlatan and his charismatic pup. Indeed, from the back of his wagon, Skorpion brought out an entire crate of bottles packed in straw. He did a brisk business, in part due to the women's saucy antics and to the first miner who, I assumed, was a plant, someone paid beforehand to stir up enthusiasm amid an audience.

Sarah smiled at the spectacle, still holding my hand. "I'll love that dog forever when he's mine."

Thinking she was being a silly kid, I said, "He's not for sale. A dog that talented is priceless."

We headed back to the wagon. I knew we had to keep heading to Virginia City in case Sarah's tribe had sent someone after us. Wounded, Bad Jace and I had seen better days. More scrapping wasn't what I needed, which was rest and money. The hydrogen wagon was a bigger headache than I'd anticipated. I didn't enjoy headaches. They turned me vicious.

Which made things unpleasant for people around me.

———

I'D DRIVEN FOR MANY, many miles that day. We had reconnected with the main trail and were drawing closer to Virginia City when Bad Jace asked me to stop for a piss and a fresh plug of tobacco. He stepped off and wandered behind some mesquite trees. Sarah, meanwhile, climbed over the top of the hydrogen tank to the rear of the wagon. I stayed in my seat, reins in my hands, waiting for the long-haired outlaw to be done so we could get rolling again. I was thinking about Poppy and how much I missed her delicious body.

Bad Jace came walking back, leaning to one side to study something behind the cart. I heard giggling and the playful sound of scampering feet. I figured Sarah was running from a butterfly or even a jackrabbit.

He stopped in front of the wagon and said, "Whose dog?"

Incredulous, I leaped down and went to inspect.

Sure enough, Sarah was throwing a stick, the dog hustling after it with manic energy.

"Sarah," I said, careful not to raise my voice. "Did you steal the doctor's puppy?"

"No," she said. She pulled her black hair from her face to give me a lovable smile. "He's decided to join us. Skorpion wasn't treating him well."

"The dog talks to you?"

She nodded.

"What's his name?"

"Typhon."

Typhon was a name in Greek mythology. Reptile son of the Titans. Interesting.

"How do you know that name, Sarah? Did the missionaries teach you?"

She shook her head and pointed at the dog, who had a stick in mouth while wagging his tail vigorously. "He told it to me."

"Someone's coming," Bad Jace said.

There was a growing dust cloud a couple miles behind us. I picked up the field glasses to see three, maybe four, horses at a steady gallop.

"This isn't an ideal place to make a stand," I said, examining the withered shrubs that surrounded us. "Pink Canyon is just ahead. If we reach it, I can hold off an army with my Sharps."

"Let's go for it," Bad Jace said, taking the glasses from me. "Closer they get, the better chance they have of blowing up our bomb on wheels."

Typhon was now jumping in the air to lick Sarah's nose, and she was giggling again.

"Back in the wagon, Sarah," I said. "Unwelcome visitors are approaching."

"They have dogs too."

Bad Jace choked on his chaw. "Kid, about what the Paiute child said? Take another look."

I took my binoculars back and trained them on the dust. There was something moving along with the horses and lower to the ground. Something that resembled bull terriers, bred for hunting slaves.

I nodded at Bad Jace.

"Eerie girl," he said.

"We're fighting bandits, Paiutes, and now slave hunters in an effort to get this wagon to Virginia City. Somehow, I don't think the hydrogen is for mere entertainment."

Bad Jace spat. "Grinaker dropped us directly into an outhouse on fire and rigged with gunpowder."

It had been years since I'd tangled with slave hunters. More than likely, the group chasing us was part of a strikebreaking outfit that boasted dog-handling skills. The idea was the same—to incite terror in and to demoralize those who refused to be hurt for the gain of others. I wasn't looking forward to the encounter. The best method for dealing with hunters and their hounds was to hit them from a distance, then cut the distance with a merciless, head-on assault.

"Take the reins," I said. "I'll use the Sharps from the baggage boot in case they catch up."

"I'm riding hard, so I don't want any complaints."

"When have I ever complained, BJ?"

He grunted, and with his good arm, pulled himself into the driver's seat.

"Okay, Sarah, let me boost you." When I stooped to pick her up, Typhon lowered his hand and growled, teeth bared.

I stopped and stood looking at the two of them.

"Sarah, Typhon is protecting you."

For no reason at all, she did a cartwheel and laughed at my hesitation. Now the dog was wagging its tail and panting, tongue out.

"He's really the best hound. I'll love him forever, remember?"

"Hyah!" Bad Jace yelled.

The horses responded, the hydrogen wagon moving. Sarah and I jumped on the back of it.

Typhon barked, got a running start, and leaped into the Paiute girl's adoring arms.

15

SUN DIPPING TOWARD THE HORIZON, WE RACED to the sandstone formations glowing vibrant shades of red. I didn't yearn for another nighttime skirmish, but if I could fend off the hunters until dark, I knew I'd be confident enough to flip the tables on them. They were getting closer, but as we passed through the mouth of the canyon, wobbling over gravel-slushed terrain and into an uncanny pink environment, I recognized a prime spot for sniping.

Wanting to hear the plan, Bad Jace brought the wagon to a stop.

"Take it all the way through!" I yelled, then took a moment to smile at Sarah and tussle her raven hair before jumping off.

"Extra rifle?" he called back.

I gave him a throat-slitting signal and pointed to my Sharps in my other hand.

Bad Jace and Sarah flinched when I rifle-blasted the baggage door chain. I unhinged and ripped the slab of reinforced oak from the wagon. It would make a decent shield. I scrambled up a sandstone arch and began assembling rocks to form a rest for the barrel of my .50 cal.

He hadn't taken off yet and I could feel his eyes on me. "See you in Virginia City, Kid."

"Watch over Sarah and Typhon. I'll catch up."

He gave me a two-fingered salute, touching the brim of his hat. Then he snapped the reins.

I watched as the girl, lying flat on her stomach atop the hydrogen container, eyes big with concern and her arm around her hijacked shepherd dog, disappeared into Pink Canyon. I had qualms about leaving Sarah with him, especially for an overnight decampment. I had no idea how his tastes in young girls ran. But I also knew that if I handled this band of hunters and took a horse from them, I'd be reunited with her and the hydrogen wagon in half a day's ride.

I flipped up my peep sight and with my field glasses ready prepared to send flying lead at the hunters the moment they came within a mile. There was wind, but not enough to discourage me from taking a shot at this distance. A red-tailed hawk soared above me, a good omen.

Gazing through my binocs, I assessed my enemy. Three riders—two of them tall and white, the third a black man. The latter seemed to be gazing straight up into the clouds, reflecting the last red rays of the setting sun, without perceiving the path before him. What did he see, I wondered.

I decided to give him an exhibition in distance shooting.

I rested the end of the barrel on the improvised tripod

of stone I'd fashioned. I wedged a rock beneath the rifle stock to measure the angle of my first shot, peered into the peep sight, and squeezed. It came off better than I'd hoped, landing a few yards ahead of the riders and nearly striking the lead dog. The dust puff erupting on the trail made them pull the reins of their horses. But this wasn't an amateur crew. Obviously, to them at least, I'd fired from the mouth of the canyon. They came at my position hard and fast, the empty desert carrying their rebel yell. I could hear, too, the pounding hooves, the barking dogs, and the arrival of violent death.

Indeed, these hunters sounded like the young men I'd known in Georgia before the war.

I loaded another round, wedged a smaller rock under the gun butt of my Sharps, and calculated for wind and the speed of their animals. I was even luckier this time, bullet-smashing the hind leg of a bull terrier. The dog yelped and tumbled into the path of one of the white riders, snag-tripping his beautiful roan, the poor creature slamming its body against the dust. The rider somer-saulted from his stirrups, landing on his back, unable to move right away. Or at all.

My third shot missed completely. I could tell this gave the hunters confidence. They were really spurring their horses to hit my position before the last ray of sunlight vanished from the sky.

My fourth shot missed too, incensing me. How in the world had I sniped them from a distance only to miss them as they got within normal range. Suddenly, I recalled that I'd never adjusted the sights with wind as a factor. I used my Bowie blade to turn the screw, adjusting for windage. I eased the front sight in the opposite direc-tion that I wanted my next bullet to go.

My fifth shot blasted the second white rider clear off

his horse with a chest-sucking wound from which there would be no recovery. However, I noticed the first rider, the one whose horse was tripped, was now up and was already grabbing the reins of his dead comrade's mount.

I had seconds to make a decision: take another shot with my Sharps or retreat into Pink Canyon for hand-to-hand combat against two mounted hunters and two dogs. Inside the canyon, I could control the distance between my enemy and me, take my time stalking the rider, lead the predator-hounds into a blind alley with a roasted sand lark, and shoot them down.

I opted to cut them down inside the canyon, using a knife and the Sharps. I scuttled down the sandstone arch, picked up the baggage door, and raced deeper into Pink Canyon.

Pink Canyon was a short, narrow, otherworldly pocket chasm used by bloodthirsty outlaws. It was the location where, years ago, a single hired killer with a single pistol had successfully fended off an entire posse of fifteen men in a Battle-of-Thermopylae-style defense that provided a small measure of fodder for New York City dime novelists. I wasn't out to recreate the grisly encounter. Rather, I had a morbid curiosity that bordered on a death wish.

I'd long wanted to die in a hail of bullets, in a place of astonishing beauty, leaving behind the most dashing corpse in the history of the American West.

IF THERE'S one thing I'd learned in my years of practicing deadly combat, armed and unarmed, it's that nothing ever goes according to plan.

The air was cool and still in Pink Canyon even as

sweat poured from my body. A few minutes of daylight remained. Waiting for the dogs, I nestled between waist-high boulders along the rim, which was twenty feet high. It didn't take long. They were soon sniffing the ground, tracking my scent. Realizing I'd scampered up the fissures and crevices of the canyon wall, they looked up, spotted me, and barked furiously. It was so much like shooting fish in a barrel that I didn't bother tossing them the sand lark. Instead, I trained my Sharps on them and prepared to pull the trigger.

Suddenly, Sarah and Typhon emerged from the opposite and upper part of the slot canyon, snagging the attention of the bull terriers.

"No!"

The hounds barked for a moment as I scrambled toward them, knowing I'd have to pull them off the girl. Losing my balance, I fell into the wash. Before I could raise my rifle through, they grew calm. I raised my head and saw that they were both peeing on rocks and eating something that the girl had in her open palm.

Breath knocked out of me from the fall, and I spit dust from my mouth. I'd also torqued my arm on a piece of limestone. I did manage, however, to ask, "What the heck are you feeding them?"

"Sidewinder jerky."

"You had food the whole time," I said.

She gave me a mischievous smile.

From around the corner came the black hunter, lean, rangy, dust-caked. Raising his gun at me, he yelled to his accomplice with his West Texas accent, "He's here!" Then to me he said, "Where's the wagon, son? You can't be the one who did all the shooting."

He had the drop on me, but I swung the baggage door

in time to deflect the rounds he fired at me from a distance of less than ten yards.

Then the three dogs suddenly blitzed him all at once, biting his gun hand, his leg, and, judging by the high-pitched sound he made, his crotch.

This gave me the chance to rush him and wallop his jaw with the knuckles of my clenched fist, knocking him into naptime. I tried to shake the sting from my hand, silently praying that I hadn't shattered the metacarpal behind my smallest finger. I didn't need a boxer's fracture.

The surviving white hunter, thinking his buddy had me pinned, came charging into the gorge on his horse, hooves crunching gravel in the wash. I was ready this time. Swinging the Sharps like a baseball bat, I smashed him in the face with the butt stock knocking him off his mount.

He went down hard, yowling.

I pushed the still-barrel against his shirt, blood-soaked from his broken nose, then slipped the pistol from his belt and shoved it into my own.

"If you don't want to die," I said, "tell me who put you on our trail."

"Guh," he replied. "My nose."

I pushed the barrel harder into his chest and he screamed. "Didn't hear you, pattyroller."

"Secretary of Nevada. You're interfering with official gummint business!"

Orion Clemens. He'd gone over my head, and around Grinaker, by hiring Texas slave hunters.

"I'm taking your guns, your dogs, and your horse. I'll leave you a canteen."

"Dogs ain't going with you."

By this time, Sarah had walked over. She stood above the flat-on-his-back hunter and stared at him. The man's dogs and Typhon followed, sniffing each other's butts, with no desire to attack the fugitives in their presence.

The man's eyes looked worried.

"I'd say they're with us," I told him, before cracking him again with a rifle butt.

I took the water skin from his horse and tossed it on the ground beside him.

I saddled up on a beautiful palomino and instructed Sarah to hop up behind me. Together with the hounds and Typhon, we walked out of Pink Canyon as the last bit of light finally faded. We had to find Bad Jace and the hydrogen wagon, then finish our journey to Virginia City.

I also needed to have words with Grinaker, Orion, and Ralston as soon as we got there.

At the end of the canyon, the valley opened up into a sky of shimmering stars and a harvest moon. It took me a few minutes to find the trail. I pushed the horse to a trot. I didn't have a timepiece, but I figured Bad Jace was intent on moving fast. Neither of us had slept well, if at all, the last two days. He likely believed Sarah and me to have been killed.

"Bad Jace," I said to Sarah, her arms tight around my gut. "He left you?"

"We left *him*," she said.

"You did?"

"Typhon and I knew you needed help."

I laughed. "I didn't save you so that you'd be killed doing something silly."

The hounds spotted something, growled, and sprinted toward it, disappearing into the darkness.

"Dogs like you," I said. "You have talent."

"I'm nice to them is all. Do you love animals?"

I looked up at the gorgeous firmament.

She yawned.

"We can't stop," I said. "Don't go to sleep or you'll fall off."

"I won't."

The hounds jogged back, without anything to show for their trouble, and trotted alongside us. In the moonlight, I saw their tongues hanging crazily from their mouths.

"There's a creek in a few miles," I said. "We'll refresh there and keep going."

True to her word, Sarah stayed awake. The brook was a lot farther away than I'd thought, but the air was cool, and the animals didn't slow down or whine. It was an enchanting ride through a quiet desert, totally unlike the coastal plains and Blue Ridge of Georgia. I didn't miss my home state—unless I was watching mining operations in Nevada, a gruesome business. Sometimes I felt terrible for the men working in those holes. A miner's life was no life, a trip into hell, a horror ripped from the Italian writer Dante's poem. They came up with grungy wheelbarrows loaded with ugly minerals that someone had decided were worth money. It made no sense to me, but then nothing really did. My mission in Virginia City was to make it easy for people to create wealth and to enrich myself in the process. With enough money, I could marry Poppy, head to California, and never do anything ugly or messy again in my life.

I saw a star falling and made a wish that I'd live long enough to realize my dream.

As we approached the ravine, I spotted a flickering campfire and heard voices. One of them sounded like Bad Jace. The other voices were men, and they didn't sound friendly.

"Sarah," I said.

"Yes?"

"Keep the dogs quiet."

"What's happening?"

"I'm about to save Bad Jace from getting himself killed."

16

WE TETHERED THE HORSE TO A JUNIPER downwind and did our best to creep up without a racket. The babbling brook, crackling fire, and loudmouthed fool smothered our approach.

"They use this here hydrogen," the bandit said, rifle pointed at Bad Jace, "to spy on Johnny Reb. In those army balloons that I read about in the newspapers."

The other bandit was inspecting the wagon, trying to make sense of the levers and hoses.

"No," Bad Jace replied, hands raised in the air. "This contraption is for entertainment purposes."

Clearly, he'd been crept up on while lighting a campfire. He couldn't see us—Sarah, me, the dogs—observing the scene behind a bundle of ponderosa pines and chokecherry shrubs. At this point, he had to be hoping that I'd killed the hunters and was on my way to him now.

The animals were on alert, ears forward, mouths closed, eyes directly engaged with the three men near the wagon.

The nosy bandit wrenched the lever, letting gas flow through the tube attached to the wagon.

Bad Jace ever-so-slightly lowered one hand to gesture to the yappy one that his foolish friend was being foolish. "He shouldn't touch that."

"What'll you do about it," said the bandit with the gun, peering at Bad Jace through crosshairs.

His reckless buddy unhooked the hose, sniffed the end of it, and, to my horror, pointed the tip of it toward the campfire.

"Not a good idea," Bad Jace warned the hose-wielding bandit.

There was ignition, fire exploding into an inferno, and the whooshing sound of oxygen abruptly consumed. The force of the detonation was startling, causing the bandit to drop the hose. But it was too late, the gas was lit. An incinerating rope of flame blasted in the direction of Bad Jace, who hit the ground, ducking a fiery guillotine. The bandit with the rifle wasn't so fortunate, his body saturated in blazing death. He was a fiery runner though, and smart enough to head toward the water. He didn't make it in time. He collapsed, spasm-writhed, and died horribly.

The bandit who ignited the blaze screamed as he came running toward us. Sarah made a noise, and the dogs careened at him like he was raw steak. He tried to raise his weapon, but the beasts knocked him flat on his butt, the bull terriers tearing into his forearms, the shepherd ripping a hole in his denim overalls. The noises that the man made were terrifying.

After picking up the bandit's pistol, I said to Sarah, "Call them off!"

She whistled, and the animals instantly stopped

chewing his limbs. They returned to her side, licking their chops like sated hellhounds.

By this time, Bad Jace had shut off the valve. The odor of cooked meat was pungent, nauseating.

I approached, and he extended his hand, eager to shake mitts. "Thanks, Kid."

I punched him hard in the windpipe, causing him to gasp for air. He fell on his knees, forehead touching the sand as the firelight flickered demonically.

"You didn't watch Sarah. Or the dog."

"His name is Typhon," Sarah corrected.

"You didn't watch Typhon."

Still on his knees, Big Jace put his hand up, indicating he needed a moment.

"We can't stop," I continued. "People in Washington are gunning for us. We need to return to Virginia City. Longer we stay out here, the more likely someone punches our tickets."

The hounds started sniffing the incinerated bandit, licking his barbecued flesh.

Bad Jace pointed at the fresh horror and vomited, splattering his clothes.

I hopped backward to avoid the splash. "Sarah, control your dogs."

She whistled sharply, and the dogs ran to her side.

I walked over to the chewed-up bandit, grabbed him by the shirt, and pulled him to his feet.

"You—you don't have to kill me."

"You came the opposite way," I said. "How many reprobates like you are searching for us on our last few miles to Virginia City?"

"A whole lot of them. From here to Washoe Lake, you're running a gauntlet."

"What's your name?"

"Goggins. Goggins Hewitt."

"Well, Goggins, you're joining us. If you keep us clear of bandits, I won't shoot you."

"I'll do—do my very best!"

"One more thing. See that patch of prickly pear?" I indicated a nearby cactus.

He nodded, eyes wet with fear.

"Grab one of those pads, slice both ends with a sharp rock, peel back the skin, and use the juice and your finger to brush your teeth in the creek there. Your breath stinks."

"Yes, sir."

I pushed him toward the cactus, and he did exactly what he was told.

"Watch him, Sarah. Don't let him grab a big rock."

"He knows better," she said, stroking one of the hounds along his spine as he growled at Goggins. "He's already been gnawed."

Bad Jace finally stood up, coughed, and rubbed his throat. "Kid," he said hoarsely, "I'll forgive you for that sucker punch if you get us back in one piece."

"Working on it. Figure we'll go through Mound House."

"How's that?"

"You heard."

"You hurt your head fighting them slave hunters."

"My head has never been clearer."

"Paiutes all through there. And ghosts"

"Sarah is Paiute. I'm half-Seminole and can pass. You can't."

Bad Jace stayed quiet.

Finally, I said, "We can't go through Washoe. Mound House is the only route."

"What'll you tell the Paiutes? And the phantoms?"

"The truth. We're avoiding federal agents. Enemy of my enemy is my friend and all that."

He sighed. "They prefer horseflesh."

"We have that now thanks to these bandits. Goggins here and Mr. Crispy."

"Should we bury him?" Sarah said.

"No time," I said. "The coyotes will clean him. Bad Jace left a few of them alive."

Sarah wrinkled her nose.

Bad Jace leaned forward, hands on his thighs like he might puke again. "Kid, anyone ever tell you you can be a tad uncaring?"

"Only when I'm fighting for my life across the Nevada desert."

———

I BOUND Goggins's hands and plopped him on his horse. Sarah and I rode the other two, and Bad Jace drove the hydrogen wagon. We took an old Paiute route that looped around Washoe and into what whites considered hostile Indian territory. I had no idea who was chief in that area at the moment, or even what tribes lived there. Smallpox had recently decimated that part of Nevada, which likely accounted for the relatively placid trek. Indeed, to our relief, there was no sniping, no aggression, no hassle—well, from Paiutes anyway.

The trouble came, as it often did, from whites. In this instance, grave robbers plundering burial sites in and around Mound House.

Mound House wasn't just the place where Northern Paiutes buried their dead. Settlers were laid to rest here too, in a solemn gravescape that emerged against the backdrop of the Sierra Nevada. The area was marked by makeshift wooden crosses and weathered stones. Unkempt wildflowers swayed in the desert breeze, adding soft melancholy to an austere landscape. A clapboard chapel, adorned with a simple cross, stood as a symbol of cherished yet forgotten solace. The wind murmured across the landscape, conjuring the haunted song of human resilience, a stark melody in honor of those who dared to carve a life in the untamed West. One day that wind would moan for my shadow, banished within the deepest pit for all of my sins, all the blood I spilled to escape the man who brought me into a world of rage and madness.

We came up on the trio of miscreants excavating a tomb; two did the hard digging while a third kept watch with a rifle. The latter was a rabid scarecrow, cloaked in an ill-fitting black suit that drew flies, staring us down with a snaggle-toothed grin and bulging eyes. He leaned on his rifle, scratching his nether regions furiously like a flea-bitten saloon mutt in need of a kerosene bath. He stared at us, simpering, reptilian, a wrecked hellspawn sulphurically erupted and famished.

The only reason I could come up with for these idiots not being slaughtered outright was that the grounds they stood on belonged to a loathed tribe no one cared to defend.

Sarah, however, was defensive, with an animal's instinct for sensing malevolence. She drew her horse close to mine, her dogs looking up at her dotingly, their tongues hanging out.

"These men," she whispered to me, "are hollow inside, like your friend Bad Jace."

"I can't risk the wagon getting damaged," I said. "Its contents are volatile."

"They'll make trouble, Crimson Boy. If we pass, they'll follow."

I said to Goggins, "Know these fellows?"

He shook his head, wiping his nose against his shirt.

"He's lying," Sarah said.

Before I could respond, the scarecrow with the rifle said, "Goggins, you with a new outfit?"

Our travel partner didn't say anything until I nudged his leg with my boot. "I certainly am, Chester! On my way to Virginia City to do that bit of bartending I'm always telling you about."

"Aha-ha," Chester mewled. "Yep, I reckon you're in it for all the free whiskey."

"Free whiskey and a life behind bars!" Goggins chuckled.

"Aha-haha. Behind *bars*. I love it!"

"Yep, it's funny!"

Then no one said anything for a moment as we made our way past the graverobbers.

"Oh hey, just one more thing before you go," said the scarecrow, raising his rifle at our caravan and sighting us through the crosshairs. "You leave Ladrón in Rattlepeak with that balloon wagon you were proselytizing to everyone about?"

"Not exact—"

Chester fired a bullet that ripped into Goggins's chest, killing him. The scarecrow was lever-actioning another around into the chamber, but Bad Jace already had his gun out.

With one hand, my long-haired companion blasted a .44 slug into Chester's shoulder. The impact knocked the scarecrow backward. He dropped his rifle and collapsed into a grave lot that he and his friends had disturbed.

Bad Jace stepped off the wagon and took his time

walking to Chester, who howled mightily in his misery. He stood above the grave robber and looked down on him, sprawled atop a wooden coffin and bleeding into the caliche and making inhuman noises. His two friends went running up the ridge, hoping to find cover on the other side.

Sarah and I saw them before Bad Jace did, but we didn't move. Not in this instance. To move would've cost us our lives. An assembly of fifteen fearsome Paiute warriors on horses had come up the ridge to finally rid Mound House of the scraggy interlopers.

They seemed to recognize the dynamics of the situation, and as the grave robbers reached the top, they were cut down by a volley of Paiute gunfire.

The warriors turned their attention to Bad Jace—who was smart enough to lower his rifle—and to Sarah and me. She waved at them, and they returned the gesture.

One warrior came down the ridge on his horse to inspect the grave Bad Jace was standing beside. He didn't like what he saw and pointed his Winchester into the trench, firing a single shot.

Then he said to us, "Everyone talks of your wagon. They say it's for balloons in Virginia City."

"Yes," I said. "And when we bring it there, we'll take you on a ride in the sky."

The warrior laughed. "I have no desire to intrude on the eagle's domain. But I'm happy to see that you stopped in Mound House to erase an evil."

The dogs growled, and Sarah hushed them with a clicking noise.

"You're the Animal Girl," the warrior said, smiling. "Sarah."

"Hello, sir," she said.

"What's your name?" I asked him.

"I am called the Cutter. And I'm escorting you to Virginia City."

"Wow, you really want to see your land from a soaring balloon," I said. "Thank you, that would be wonderful."

"I should see it," he said, still smiling, "before you, and men like you, take it and everything else from us."

"I won't take anything from you, Cutter. I'm leaving here as soon as I save enough money."

He studied me for a moment. "You won't be leaving. I see a shadow."

"Shadow of death?"

"No," he said. "Something darker."

17

THE CUTTER AND HIS WARRIORS TOOK US ALL the way to the city limits, then galloped away without a word. Bad Jace pulled the hydrogen wagon right up to the Dead Dice Saloon. We looked like we'd survived Gettysburg—cut, bruised, bleeding. A crowd started gathering as soon as we arrived. I heard someone say, "Is that Kid Crimson? He looks beat to hell."

It was true I'd seen better days. But there was satisfaction in getting an impossible job done and done well. I didn't believe in performing menial tasks and finding nobility in them. I'd scrubbed more outhouses and swept more floors than anyone alive, what I'd done in between fights on the child-boxing circuit in the South. I preferred to operate on an epic scale, what being a hired gun allowed me to do. As an adult, I strove to make my life a heroic, if chaotic, poem penned by Homer or Virgil. The best way to end this piece of verse was to die young and pretty in a hail of bullets or to live a long, contented life in a luscious grapefruit orchard in California.

I was working toward the latter option, but if I was

honest with myself, the former worked for me just as well.

And if, along the way, I could save my friends from being harmed by others, from being mauled by their own petty desires and self-destructive whims, I'd be a happy man.

I intended to go straight to Grinaker, but he greeted us outside in an effort, I thought at the time, to discourage me from taking a swing at him in public.

It didn't work. I didn't bother tying up my horse. I dismounted and headed right toward him, pushing my way through the curious onlookers, causing them to curse at me.

Grinaker didn't back down. He wore a salty look even as I got within strangulation range. That's because his security man, Butenhoff, was there to put me in a full nelson, latching his arms under my armpits with his hands pushing against my neck. I struggled like a netted fish, but I was too exhausted, too dehydrated, to wrestle free. Bad Jace didn't know that and slipped my pistol from my belt; he'd seen the monster unleashed. When I raised my knee to try to stomp Butenhoff's boot, I felt dizzy.

"Grinaker," I said. "I'm not thrilled."

He kept smiling his repulsive smile. "No, I don't suppose you are. But your friend Chaparral will be ecstatic. So will his Mormon courtesan, who sees the future in a rock."

Sarah's dogs growled. She squatted beside them to prevent them from wrapping their jaws around the saloon owner's neck.

Grinaker eyed her. "You've made friends."

"*Your* friends, though, Orion Clemens and Ralston," I

said, trying to wriggle free, "are up to something. I'll find out what."

"You're tired, Kid. Take a rest. We'll discuss it when you feel better."

"I feel good enough to whoop you into next week. Your birth certificate is as good as canceled." I heard my old Georgia accent worming its way into my voice.

The edges of my vision clouded. I was growing dangerously faint. But then I saw my beautiful Poppy there to help me. Chaparral and Jericho showed up, too, which allowed Butenhoff the chance to slowly release me into their care. I couldn't stand on my own, my friends encouraging me to lean on them for support. They guided me, boots dragging the dust, to Grover's office.

"Come on, Kid," Chaparral said. "We'll address this nonsense in the morning. Rest for you."

"Scullard," I said.

"What about him?"

"Don't let that drunken sawbones near me."

"He won't touch you," Jericho promised. "He won't so much as *look* at you."

"Kid," Poppy said, kissing my brow, which I couldn't even raise at this point, "I can't believe you made it. We heard awful stories!"

"All garbage," Jericho said. "I knew they couldn't put you in the ground."

"I owe you, Kid," Chaparral said. "Rosie's so happy to have her peepstone back."

"He doesn't look good," Poppy said. "Can you please hurry? He needs to lie down. I'm going to fetch him some water."

"He's fine," Jericho said. "He's the Kid."

"I looked into the claim you gave me," Chaparral said.

"The worthless one from Vestrick. It has zero value, yes, but there's something that you'll find interesting. The claim is located directly adjacent to the Ophir stamp mill."

"So what? I managed to say. "I need to lie down."

"Almost there. I started thinking... There's a lot of unused quicksilver stored in that mill."

"Poisonous stuff. I don't recommend drinking it."

"Yes, but I hear it cures syphilis. Anyhow, the quick-silver has been sitting there for a few years now, and I don't think too many people recall that."

"And?" My throat was burning at this point.

"Well, Vestrick gave you the claim for a reason. He's British. He thinks things through."

"Yes. I need a drink of water."

Right at that moment, Poppy jogged back with the ladle from a nearby well. The water was cool, refreshing. I immediately felt better.

"And then I overheard that fellow Orion chatting with Ralston."

"I'm sure. Important visitor coming soon."

"Yes, well, they plan to bring that important visitor through Ophir."

I planted my feet to the ground now, ready to walk of my own accord, and reached into my coat for a handker-chief. There was none to be had. I said nothing, just stared at Chaparral, my mind beginning to work again.

"In other words," he said, lowering his voice, "it's the worst place to bring President Lincoln."

"Wow," I said. "Who owns the old stamp mill?"

"Grinaker."

That didn't sound good. "We should ask Vestrick why he transferred the claim to me."

"We can't do that."

"Why not?"

Chaparral looked at Jericho. Jericho looked at Poppy. Poppy looked at me, her lovely visage tinged with concern.

"Vestrick was killed last night."

———

POPPY PREPARED A HOT, soothing bath in a claw-footed tub cascading with pink and red rose petals. Her room above the Sure Cure was a lavish, soap-scented escape from Virginia City's grimy streets. Her windows were big, bringing in the crisp sun and blue sky of Nevada. After a soak, I took a desperately needed nap, sleeping three hours with Poppy's fragrant head on my chest. At dusk, she asked if I was hungry. I said I was ravenous. She left and, minutes later, brought me a still-hot caramelized pork chop from a Chinatown food stall, so good it made my tongue want to slap my brains out. I used my hands instead of a knife and fork, bolting it down.

"I brought vegetables," Poppy insisted.

"No thanks," I said.

"My carnivore boyfriend. My proud lion."

I growled in her ear, and she giggled.

We abandoned the food on her red lacquer dinner table and migrated back to the bed to hold each other close. We didn't make love; instead, we listened to each other's heartbeat, running our fingers through each other's hair. Her breath smelled like ginger tea and almond cookies. I wanted to kiss her lips forever. She was a beautiful dream from which I never wanted to wake.

I had to get some answers, though. Being with her for a few hours was a delicious recharge, but it was time to figure out what was happening, who was conspiring, and why.

"So no idea who's responsible?"

She turned away from me to stare at her bedroom ceiling. "Vestrick had just left the Sure Cure. He'd been here all day and into the evening. He mentioned to me that his room in the Gold Hill Hotel had been torn up, robbed. Someone was looking for something, he said."

"Did he say what they were looking for?"

She sat up, fluffing the pillow before nestling it behind her shoulders, between her spine and the head-board. She took my hand in her own, examining my scarred knuckles. "No. For whatever reason, he didn't seem to care. He acted as if the people responsible would never find what they wanted. He acted like he didn't care if they returned or found him alone. You know, Kid, I wanted..." She closed her eyes, tears flowing.

"What did you want, Flower?"

"I wanted to help him," she said, "to soothe his wounds from the Arrow War. You know, Kid, he was one of the men. The terrible men who..." She grabbed the sheets, pulled them over her head before emitting a sob.

"I know, Flower. He was with the British navy when they destroyed the city of Canton, where you lived as a child."

"What the world does to boys," she said, dabbing her eyes with the edge of the bedsheet. "It's unforgivable."

"What boys do to the world isn't good, either." Of course, I knew what she meant. She was saying that, in war, everyone is brutalized, broken, and made inhuman. I escaped Georgia to leave the War between the States behind me. It stalked me for thousands of miles, all the way to Virginia City, to Rattlepeak, to Mound House, to Pink Canyon. Armed conflict was inevitable; the more you ran from it, the harder it followed. Even man's less violent, simplistic efforts to get rich through silver mining depended entirely on a market manipulated by a militarized nation, by a once-promising country burning itself alive in a furnace of self-inflicted bloodshed.

Poppy went on. "I thought the Sure Cure might help treat the anger inside Vestrick."

I should've stayed quiet and listened. Instead, I said, "There's no healing."

"He resigned himself to dying, to being killed. Makes me think you're right. We can't be fixed."

I redirected. "You heal me, Flower. Right here and now, I'm restored. You mend me."

"Am I enough for you, Kid?" She touched my chin.

"You are. Did Vestrick mention the claim he gave me?"

Poppy shook her head.

"Have Chaparral and Jericho told you what they think?"

"No, they've shared nothing with me. But Vestrick *did* enjoy a last meal at the Blood Nugget. That woman who owns the place, who's in love with you, might know something."

Poppy meant Verbena. I tabled my girlfriend's comment. "I'll check with her later. First, I need to see Grover and take a look at Vestrick's corpse."

"I can't say," she said, "that Grover looked surprised when we told him."

"Nothing surprises an undertaker in Virginia City. In a place rampant with silver ore, no one can afford a coffin or a proper burial."

"Ralston is paying for Vestrick's funeral."

"Interesting. I'll speak with Ralston too, at some point."

"The sun will be setting soon, Kid." She pulled me into her arms and kissed me. "I'll help you get ready." She gently pushed me away and leaped out of bed. She was slender, nymph-like. I watched her slip on her stockings and fell madly in love with her all over again.

I pulled her back into bed and she squealed.

"Poppy," I said, "would you ever consider running away with me?"

"Where?" She made a donut bun from her long black hair, using a hairpin to hold it in place.

"California. Sonoma County."

"What will we do there?"

"I don't know. Thinking about a grapefruit orchard."

She left the bed again to study herself in the full-length mirror. "Kid, I didn't know you wanted to be a farmer."

"I can't keep doing this forever, Flower. I want to fill you with babies and grow old with you."

"Let me know when you're ready," she said, retrieving a set of freshly laundered clothes and my boots that Ezra had cleaned for me.

"You'll leave with me? When the time comes?"

She kissed my cheek. "I have a thriving business here. I can't just walk away."

I sat at the edge of the bed, my back to her. I stared at the carpet on the floor of her room.

"Let's go, Kid. We should see Grover before he closes up his office for the day."

I couldn't move, felt frozen in place.

"Kid?"

"Grover is going to be very busy in the coming weeks. His office won't close anytime soon."

"Do you plan on giving him plenty of work?"

I stood up, kissed her passionately, and put on my clothes she'd laundered for me.

18

THE WEATHERED SIGN CREAKED OVERHEAD, bearing the ominous yet comforting words: Grover's Graveside Services.

The door swung open with a groan, revealing a dimly lit interior that smelled of polished wood, varnish, and embalming fluids. Caskets of varying sizes dominated the space, each a repository for the soon-to-be-departed. The flickering light of oil lamps cast weird shadows.

Grover's desk, cluttered with paperwork and faded photographs of stoic faces, served as the nerve center of this melancholy operation. Quill pens and inkwells rested alongside ledgers detailing the names and fates of the deceased. He was always writing in a large, leather-bound ledger that contained meticulous records of services rendered—a macabre account of lives extinguished on the rugged frontier.

I knew where I'd find him, in the corner, behind a bamboo partition that obscured a makeshift embalming room, where he practiced the delicate art of preserving the departed. Bottles of chemicals and medical instruments adorned a worn table. Grover always displayed a sense of reverence and respect for the deceased, including the most gratuitous alcoholics and cold-blooded killers. He treated every corpse that arrived on his doorstep in the same solemn manner. When I first met Grover a few years ago, his office was a zone of meditation, introspection, where the stark realities of life and death converged, People yearned for solace in the arms of Grover, who prepared their loved ones for their final journey into the unknown. He was more than a mortician; he was a comforter to the grief-stricken.

I was the first killer Grover knew. He comforted me, because he fathomed the reasons why I turned out the way I did. He consoled me, I suspected, because he believed me to be already dead, that it was only a matter of time before a gravedigger shoveled a trench in the ground for me to sleep in forever. Grover never judged me, which is why he became my surrogate father in Virginia City. He was the first man older than me who had accepted me for what I was. He didn't try to shape me into a reflection of his own mangled ego. Perhaps he understood where it was that we all end up and figured that changing me wouldn't amount to a hill of beans.

"Grover," I said to the shadow behind the partition, knowing he'd be working on the body. "I'm here with Poppy."

He stepped out into the light, wiping his hands on a rag. "Poppy! Good to see you, ma'am."

"Hello, Grover," she said, grabbing my arm. "Can you believe Kid made it back?"

"Mr. Crimson is a difficult man to thwart when he puts his mind to something."

"Although," I said, "I'm a man vexed, apparently. I hear Ralston paid for Vestrick's funeral."

"Yes. Does that interest you, Kid?"

"Not yet. Mind if I take a look at the old Brit?"

"It's against my policy, Kid."

"Obviously, Grover. But this is job-related."

Grover nodded, knowing what I was referring to. He walked to the entrance and flipped the sign to CLOSED. "Poppy, care for a drink?"

"That sounds wonderful, Grover."

While they sipped whiskey and chatted about the looming miners' strike and how it might affect business, I went behind the partition to inspect Vestrick.

He was naked with a white towel around his waist. He looked peaceful and unblemished, like he was simply taking a rewarding snooze. I twisted a metal dial on one of the lamps to expose the wick and generate more light.

The hole was in his right temple, just above his ear. Grover had removed the bullet. The cartridge was in a small metal pan, sitting in a splash of blood. I grabbed some forceps to pick up the slug so I could examine it closely. It was a 10mm, and I only knew of a few Derringer owners in town—one of them being, interestingly, Ralston. I'd last seen it on him when he opened his jacket to pay for breakfast at the Griddle of Doom ten days prior.

Then again, Grinaker had one, too. Did it shoot 10mm?

I poured rubbing alcohol on a towel, wiped the bullet clean, and dropped it into my coat pocket.

I was about to leave when I noticed something glinting beneath Vestrick's fingernails. I carefully lifted his hand to inspect the shiny-white compound. Quicksilver. Grover usually performed manicures on his corpses, so he might've noticed the substance. But if bodies piled up and he got busy, maybe not. I didn't know what this detail meant exactly, but it related to what Chaparral had discovered in his investigation of the claim that Vestrick had drunkenly bestowed on me.

I washed my hands in the basin and walked into the coffin display to find them still talking.

"Find what you're looking for?" Grover said.

"Maybe," I said. "Should we all grab dinner?"

"I have to keep working. Funeral is tomorrow."

"Too bad." I turned to Poppy. "Are you saying a few words?"

She nodded. "I'm reciting his favorite poem."

"Let me guess, Shelley's 'Ozymandias.'"

"Yes! Thank goodness it's a short verse. I hope I pronounce everything correctly."

"You'll do fine," Grover assured.

At that moment, someone knocked at the door.

"We're closed!" Grover boomed. "Wait, I think it's Ezra."

When the door was unlocked and opened, the shoeshine boy rushed in, pulling me by my sleeve.

"Kid, you have to come now!"

"What happened?" I said.

"It's the Animal Girl. She's beguiled all the wild dogs in town. They're pushing over garbage cans along the alley that runs behind restaurant row and causing a ruckus."

"What happened to Chaparral? He's supposed to be watching her!"

"He was. But when Sarah gathered all the beasts, they bowled him over and he bonked his head on a hitching post outside the Blood Nugget."

"The piano player can't suffer a head injury. He's the only decent saloon musician in the entire state. Poppy, can you please fetch Dr. Scullard?"

"Why," she said, arms crossed, "do you always insist on calling Scully for everyone else's injuries but never for your own?"

"I'm scared of getting amputated by that notorious inebriate. You see, with other people's limbs, I don't feel the same sense of peril."

Ezra looked at me askance, then said to Poppy, "Well, he admitted it."

————

It was as Ezra explained. Sarah held sway over a dozen trash-subsisting mutts in the shriveled heart of Virginia City, plus the three dogs that had joined her during her escape from Ash Creek. The animals ran roughshod, vexing people enough that a miner drew a pistol and tried to shoot one of them. It didn't work, and he was bitten pretty badly. The incident had already drawn the attention of John Mackay, superintendent of the biggest mining operation in Nevada. He was assembling a posse to exterminate the beasts, luring men like Bad Jace with greenback dollars.

He emerged from the Dead Dice Saloon with four men in tow. His buddies had obviously been drinking whiskey to steel up their nerve to shoot defenseless pooches.

I showed up in time to mute his flaring temper. "Bad Jace, really? Back in town less than twenty-four hours, having barely survived attacks by bandits, Paiutes, and gravediggers, and you've already signed up for some puppy-culling."

"Come on, Kid," he said. "Sarah is winding up every mutt from here to Sun Mountain. Town is crazy enough with booze, women, and cards. Last thing we need in the mix is wild dogs."

"Borrowed pistols isn't a good idea, either. I'll take mine back now, thank you."

Bad Jace sighed, pulled from his belt the gun he'd taken from me yesterday, and handed it to me.

"Thanks," I said. "Now let's move these curs out of the city limits. Here comes Jericho now."

"The bartender?"

I started walking to one end of C Street, and Bad Jace and his bunch of hesitant dog-slaughterers reluctantly followed.

I'd asked the Blood Nugget whiskey-slinger to bring Verbena's caged wagon to the end of the alley that ran behind the eateries and saloons. I came over and unlatched the cargo door, which exposed the pile of beef scraps Poppy had secured from her cousin Sing's noodle house.

I whistled sharply. Suddenly, around the corner, at the alley's midpoint, the mutts came stampeding at me, like the Charge of the Hound Brigade, the scent of meat remnants in the air, triggering their salivary glands. When they had all jumped inside the wagon for a tasty bite of beef tongue, balls, and brains, I slammed the cage door shut and locked it. The dogs fought over the offal, snarling and tussling.

Bad Jace guffawed loudly. "Kid, you're ridiculous. But also kind of a genius."

His mirth caused the men that were with him to laugh, too.

"What a relief," said one of them. "I wasn't looking forward to shooting a dog." He and the rest of the men, including Bad Jace, began making their way back to the Dead Dice.

I walked around to Jericho in the driver's seat and shook hands with him.

"Take them to the scrapyard?" Jericho confirmed.

"Yes, I said. "Poppy's uncle set up a pen there for them. It's got a freshwater pump and old couch beds."

"Maybe *I* should move in there."

"Always an option."

"Uh-oh, Kid," Jericho warned. "Here she comes. I'll be seeing you!" He snapped the reins.

Scowling, unblinking, Sarah walked toward me in dramatic fashion with short, quick steps, arms straight down and fists clenched to indicate her unhappiness.

She tried to plod her way through me, and it was almost adorable. But no one, not even a child, pushes Kid Crimson. I removed my cowboy hat, moved to the side, and swatted the back of her head with the brim, startling her.

"I'm not your father, but if you don't stop this nonsense right now, you *will* get spanked."

"My dogs did nothing wrong. They have nothing to eat here. People in Virginia City are mean!"

"Welcome to so-called civilization," I said. "Cease your worries, Sarah. We found a place for them that's nicer than the Gold Hill Hotel, and you can visit them any time. Heck, you can stay there with them if you want."

"Really?" she said, eyes bright with anticipation. "Where?"

"Less than half a mile away, next to the scrapyard at the edge of Sun Mountain."

"They'll get fat!" she said, rubbing her hands together with delight. "Fat like pigs!"

"Speaking of pigs," I said, "I need you to ride out there with me and talk to them."

She furrowed her brow. "I don't want to talk with my food."

"Not baconers. I need you to meet the gunpowder hogs of Virginia City."

"What are those?"

"They're pigs that Poppy's uncle John John trained to sniff out gunpowder in his Chinatown poker rooms."

"Why gunpowder?"

"John John had a no-firearms-at-the-table policy to discourage cheaters and stick-up artists. Last winter his place burned down in a fire. He's been renting out his pigs to mining operators to detect gunpowder left behind by previous digs."

"Why do they need to find gunpowder?"

"Sometimes a defunct company or rival outfit will leave behind a few sticks in the shaft, which are hard to see in the dark. To keep from getting blown up, a mine company will send one of Sing's pigs into the hole."

"A life-saving porker!"

"Exactly. Care to meet them?"

"I'd love that!"

"Great! There's a condition, however."

"Tell me."

"You're not allowed to foment a pig rebellion."

She put her hands on her hips, indignant. "Now why would I do that?"

"Seriously, Sarah. It's life or death when it comes to gunpowder."

"I'll be serious and helpful. Ready to hear my condition?"

"Sure."

"Tell Ezra he should teach me how to shine shoes with him."

"You're not getting along?"

"Oh yes, we get along great! It's just that—well, he says no wife of his is going to work."

"Um, aren't you both ten years old?"

"Yes, so?"

"Nothing," I said, removing my hat to scratch my head. "I'll talk to him about it."

19

Poppy's uncle was John John, a Manchu diplomat, exiled and nearly executed by the Heavenly Kingdom rebels for being a British spy. He'd made his way to San Francisco then went east to work as a railroad worker before settling in Virginia City as a swineherd and restaurateur. His farm brought back memories. As a boy, pigsties were bustling, odorous places for combat training. I was all too familiar with them in Georgia. A big part of my father's cruel training regimen involved making me chase hogs caked in red clay and feces. I had to pin them down so they couldn't break free from my grasp. If I failed, I was trampled, kicked, and bitten. Those were just the injuries my father inflicted. Unsuccessfully pinned hogs wreaked all kinds of havoc. I had to be careful not to lose a finger or an ear in their agitated, gnashing jowls. I imagined that this explained why I relished eating pig meat. Wolfing down a ham steak was, for me, an act of delicious revenge.

Surrounded by scraggly olive trees and vegetable patches—broccoli, cabbage, cauliflower—John John's farm consisted of a group of rickety wooden structures, including a farmhouse, barn, and pigsty constructed from repurposed materials. The earth around the farm bore the marks of hard work, with patches of tilled soil and well-worn paths leading to various outbuildings. A motley crew of hogs, hides splattered with mud, foraged for sustenance. The grunts and squeals of pigs mixed with the clucks of chickens, creating a cacophony that echoed through the dry, still air.

John John didn't seem convinced I was really in the market for a gunpowder-sniffing pig.

"You're not a miner," he said, frowning at me in his work pants and black leather boots that went over his knees. "You're a killer. Why do you need pigs?"

"I'm paying you a lot of money," I said, "not to ask that question."

John John huffed and walked over to the pen. Before he opened the gate, he looked at Sarah and said, "These aren't friendly pets for you to feed cookies to on the furniture."

"She's a wizard child from the wilderness, John John," I said. "She's no city slicker from the Tenderloin."

He considered her again and shook his head. He unlocked the pigsty, waving us to follow.

Sarah bristled, but walked into the pen, and I accompanied her. When we were inside, the pigs that had been scavenging on the other side of the pen suddenly grew quiet with our presence.

John John had urged Sarah to wear adult boots that didn't fit her. They were awkward yet kept her feet out of the muck. She golem-clomped toward the pigs, arms extended.

"Oink," she said, smiling.

The biggest of the animals pricked up his ears, snorted, and approached.

"That's King Zhou," John John said.

"Does he bite?" I asked.

"They all do."

"No," Sarah said, pulling a sliced apple from her overalls. "They're content now."

King Zhou came close, curled his lips to expose his front teeth, and pushed his snout against Sarah's booted foot. He huff-snorted until he began to make a gagging sound. Sarah laughed from the warm tickle of his breath and stroked his back. King Zhou seemed at ease, relaxed.

She fed him an apple slice, and another, which he accepted carefully, affectionately. The other pigs saw and heard what was happening and came over to join in the snacking. Sarah gave each of the pigs a piece of apple.

"Their tongues tickle my fingers," she said.

"How do we get them to find gunpowder?" I asked.

"With this." John John presented us with a collar and leash, like you'd put on a dog. "You walk the animals through an area. When they locate a gunpowder stash, they snort and scratch. That's when you give them a treat."

"They like fruit," Sarah said.

John John nodded. "King Zhou is the best at this."

"Why isn't he being used now?" I asked.

"Mine operators have an ultimatum this week. Produce ore quickly or get shut down."

"Who'd shut them down?"

"US government."

"Wait, so they want fewer safety conditions this week, of all weeks?"

"My pigs," John John said, "aren't a recognized safety precaution. Superintendent John Mackay brings them down into the mines before sending his men into a shaft built by a previous company. It's rare that they find anything down there. My pigs were better at sniffing guns on card cheats in my poker room before it burned down."

I considered asking him if he thought that had been a case of arson but decided to stick with the subject at hand.

"Let's put your swine to the test," I said. "I dropped a bullet in the muck as we made our way across the pen. Can they find it?"

John John indicated that Sarah should leash King Zhou, but she refused. Instead, she walked with the alpha pig in the direction from which we came.

"King Zhou," she said. "Find me the bang-bang bullet."

"She's a talker," John John said to me.

The pig wandered around the middle of the pigsty, smelling the muck, stopping here and there to zero in on an interesting scent before moving to a different spot. I wasn't impressed and didn't think the dumb animal would find anything save his own flatulence. But then, all at once, something happened in his little swine brain. King Zhou started getting excited, circling the area where I recalled dropping the bullet and kicking a clump of mud over it. Suddenly, he emitted a raspy squeal and scratched at the site. Sarah reached down to extract it, raising it into the air in her fist. The pig started bumping into her intentionally, so she reached into her overalls again to feed him another piece of fruit.

John John uncrossed his arms and pinch-stroked the ends of his mustache. "I see now why they call her Animal Girl. She'd be perfect for my processing facility."

"You can't put a ten-year-old girl to work in your

slaughterhouse, John John," I said. "She'd turn the creatures against you. You'd have a full-blown Jules Verne novel on your hands."

Instead of smiling, he seemed to give this serious thought. Then he said, "What are your intentions with my niece?"

"I'll marry Poppy and take her to Sonoma County to plant a grapefruit orchard."

"What about Ezra and this Animal Girl?"

"What about them?"

"Will they be your children and Poppy's?"

I hadn't thought that part all the way through. "Sure, why not. Anything wrong with them?"

We both looked at Sarah, who was smooch-kissing King Zhou directly on the snout.

John John sighed, shook his head again. "I fear for their generation."

"Me, too, John John."

―――――

THE NEXT DAY, at the top of Mount Ophir, Grinaker was ready to launch his "entertainment" into the air. It was a dazzling sight to behold. Poppy and her cousin Sing had done a magnificent job sewing together silk sheets, dresses, and curtains to create a colossal balloon of shimmering fabric. It billowed as the hot air, from roaring flames beneath, brought it to swelling life. The vibrant, multicolored dirigible contrasted with the blue sky above, cloudless and divine. The gondola, suspended beneath the balloon and anchored to the ground by the strength of Bad Jace and Butenhoff, held its first Virginia City passengers—Verbena, Ralston, Mackay—faces alight with trepidation and excitement. Grover had set up his tintype camera to document the event. The hydrogen wagon was off to the side, sitting at the ready to fuel the burners.

I hadn't yet asked Grinaker or Ralston about what the slave hunters had said to me. This was as good a chance as any to clear up everything.

Orion Clemens's brother, the journalist Samuel Clemens, was there too, scribbling into his notepad, an ironic smirk on his face.

"Drag the miners into a hellish pit and pay them a few dollars," he witticized. "Shoot them into heaven for the same price. Grinaker is a business genius or an overzealous reader of Dante."

"He's a Virginia City scoundrel," I said. "Present company excluded, this town lures neither geniuses, nor fans of Florentine verse."

"You could be right. Killers and crackpots seem to be in long supply here. And no one owns a library card. Present company excluded."

I laughed. "Will this balloon test serve as the subject of your first published *Territorial Enterprise* article?"

"If it soars. If it crashes, I worry the incident may cast a pall over my literary ambitions."

"You have artistic dreams. Curious that you choose to ignite them in such a rugged place."

"It's the perfect canvas," Sam Clemens said. "Where else can you watch a beautiful angel down a whiskey shot before soaring into the sky with toadish men in suits and top hats?"

Something about what he said irked me, though it shouldn't have. Verbena wasn't my lover. She was my employer and good friend. Still, her maternal presence in my life wasn't as chaste as I liked to think. I swallowed my anger for the moment, and said, "Mr. Clemens, you'll never want for a tale as tall as the Winder Building as long as you're in Virginia City."

"Kid!" Verbena called out to me from the wicker basket as Ralston chatted with Grinaker, who was operating the gas. "Don't let me go up alone with these men! Join me, my dark prince!"

Clemens seemed to find this amusing. He chuckled as I tightened the drawstring on my hat.

I went running toward her, bounding into the gondola with too much momentum, nearly spilling us all into the dirt. Managing to regain our balance, Verbena and I laughed and held each other tight. My stomach sank a little when I realized that Bad Jace and Butenhoff were the ones responsible for releasing us into the wind. But they were too focused on the task at hand, faces blank with anxiety, to plot any mischief. Grinaker, meanwhile, exuded confidence.

"Don't worry," he said. "We're safer than grandma's cornbread and buttermilk. Sit back and enjoy the debut ride of Grinaker's Skyrider Services!"

We all laughed at this, since there was no place to sit. We laughed harder when Ralston passed us a whiskey flask that was undoubtedly less safe than buttermilk.

The hiss of escaping steam and the pulsing of the gas burners signaled that we were about to defy gravity. With a sudden surge, the balloon gently lifted off the ground. The sensation it gave me was akin to the buoyancy of a dream.

The balloon ascended. The landscape unfurled beneath us like a grand tapestry. The serenity of flight enveloped us as the world below transformed into miniature vignettes of life. Vast canyons and winding rivers blossomed into Washoe Lake. Distant mountains loomed majestically on the horizon. The air, crisp and invigorating, carried the sounds of terra firma in a muted symphony. The promise of boundless possibility was in the gondola, and beyond; we all felt it.

The anger that I had intended to share with Ralston and Grinaker softened amid cotton-ball clouds and the gondola's gentle sway.

"How high up are we?" I asked.

"One-thousand feet," Grinaker said, turning a dial on the burner to add gas to the balloon.

Ralston used his field glasses to survey the earth.

"It's so beautiful," Verbena said softly, holding me tight.

I thought about all the blood and gore that another had spilled for the simple pleasure of this thrill ride. Dead Dobie, the killings of Stoner Kurgin and his gang in Rattlepeak, the madness of Sarah's Paiute chief, the slave hunters, the bandits, the graverobbers, the Cutter and his crew. So much death, and all for a gorgeous bird's-eye view and a kiss from a lovely older woman.

I gripped an upright to ensure our balance; I grabbed Verbena's waist with my other hand, pulling her closer to my body.

"Kid," she said. "Kiss me. In case we fall from the sky and die, I want you to kiss me."

I did what I was told. I was a good boy, after all. She tasted like the delicious candy that I used to buy from the pharmacy in Macon. I paid for the candy with coins I'd earned from fighting other boys in the creeks and marshes outside the city while men watched, laughing and eager to see blood, to see kids hurt one another. Later, they tried to hurt us themselves.

I kissed Verbena a bit too fervidly, but she didn't seem to mind. She made a whimpering noise, then broke it off. "God, that was good. I might ask you to do that again."

"Maybe later," I said. "I need to chat with our fellow passenger and the pilot of this ship."

We went back to watching the landscape and holding each other snugly. A gust of wind moved us back in the direction of Mount Ophir. Ralston withdrew his binoculars and looked at me.

"You made all this possible, Kid," he said. "I see why Grinaker here tasked you with securing the hydrogen. This will be an impressive feature for the visit we have planned in a few days."

"Thanks, Ralston," I said. "You know, something funny happened when I was interrogating a slave hunter who'd drawn a bead on the hydrogen wagon."

I could feel Verbena stiffen beside me. I knew she was worried I might toss Ralston—maybe Grinaker, too—from the balloon if I didn't get the answers I wanted.

Ralston stayed silent for a moment, resting his elbow on the edge of the gondola, crossing one leg over the other. "Only you could find something funny, Kid, during an attack by slavers."

Grinaker, despite not having his bodyguard Butenhoff present, didn't act concerned. He was, however, looking at me to see what came next.

"The slave hunter insisted that he was conducting 'official government business,'" I said. "Got me thinking that, when I told you I had a job with Grinaker, you or that fellow Orion might've sent word. Or maybe it was Grinaker here that sent them after me."

"You're forgetting about Dobie," Grinaker said. "The man I hired to bring the hydrogen wagon out west—well, he just wasn't trustworthy. He ran his mouth. A lot. Bad

Jace spent two days drinking with that Dobie fellow. Bad Jace would know."

"It didn't feel right out there," I said. "The part about 'government business' bothers me."

"He meant the Confederacy," Grinaker said.

"What?"

"The Confederate government of President Jefferson Davis. In Richmond, Virginia."

"He's right," Ralston insisted. "The slave hunter from Texas was referring to the government that he recognizes, the government that hired him to retrieve the wagon for Johnny Reb."

I hadn't thought of that. I had to admit it was a possibility.

"What kind of bullet does your Derringer take, Mr. Grinaker?"

"Ten mm. Why?"

"That's exactly the cartridge that Grover pulled from Vestrick's dead head." I pulled the bullet from my jacket and tossed it at him.

He caught it and handed it to Ralston, who inspected it with two hands, bringing it close to his face with a squint.

"I use the same caliber in my gun," Ralston said.

Grinaker sighed. "I realize it was a strenuous job, not at all what you envisioned. That's why I put a bonus in your account yesterday. Next time you're at the bank, take another look at your balance."

"Thanks, Grinaker."

"Let's head back now," he said. "Before we drift away to paradise and never return to Virginia City."

Ralston laughed. "Can we vote on it?"

The two of them began talking about a technical

aspect of balloon travel when Verbena tugged on my coat.

"Now's not a good time," she whispered in my ear, "but later we should chat about Vestrick."

I nodded.

"What do you think of the view, Kid?"

"I think it's splendid. Very inspiring."

"What does it inspire you to want to do? Throw old, rich men off a balloon to watch them fall?"

"It inspires me," I said, "to grow wings and fly out of Virginia City."

"But the money, Kid. Grinaker says he put more into your account."

"Yes," I said. "Money is a gilded birdcage for a raven like me."

"Tweet for me, Raven."

"Ravens don't tweet; they gurgle-croak."

Verbena considered this. "I'd prefer you kiss me, then."

And I did.

20

GRINAKER GOT US DOWN SAFELY NEAR THE BASE of Mount Ophir. After our adventure and Grover's photo shoot, the collective enthusiasm over the balloon dissipated. Bad Jace and Butenhoff broke down the amusement ride, opening the deflation port, folding up the silk, and packing onto a wagon. People were in a festive mood and distracted as they headed back to town. Jericho and I took the opportunity to investigate Vestrick's mining rights.

Just like Chaparral had said, the claim was located adjacent to the abandoned Ophir stamp mill. Vestrick owned a tunnel site that obviously clenched up, yielding no more silver after a point. I'd heard that, before my arrival to Virginia City, Vestrick had struck a rich vein, making thousands in a few months' time, enough to spend his days at the Sure Cure without ever having to work again. It was evident no one had been working on-site for some time. There was an absence of tools, and no evidence of cooking or campfire debris.

There were, however, boot tracks leading from the mouth of the tunnel to the stamp mill.

"See this?" I said to Jericho.

"I do," he said. "I have lamps."

He lit the wicks. Together we walked into the darkness of dead Vestrick's dried-up mine.

A scorpion scuttled into a crevice. Otherwise, nothing moved other than ourselves. The boot tracks were easy to follow, along with what seemed to be wheelbarrow marks. We didn't have to duck or stoop, suggesting this was a site that Vestrick had sunk significant funding into, at least initially, back when it produced ore. We pushed at least twenty yards into the cave when we found a container of what I assumed was tools or mining equipment. Jericho squatted directly in front of the aluminum box to illuminate with his lamp the initials someone had painted there: *Q.S.*

"Quicksilver," I said. "Mercury."

Jericho used his knife to pop open the lid. He dipped a finger into the liquid inside and tasted it. "Sweet. Metallic."

"Careful," I said. "That stuff makes miners lose their minds."

"I work as a bartender in Virginia City," he said, wiping mercury on his pants. "I can confirm."

"What's this barrel here?"

"I can smell it from here. Alcohol."

"All I smell is urine," I said.

"Yes, someone's storing that too."

"Disgusting."

"It's not normal. Even for mercury-poisoned miners."

I couldn't figure it out. "Vestrick was further gone than I knew."

"Mercury," Jericho said, reciting an equation. "Grain alcohol. Urine."

There was a clattering noise outside the mine. We looked at each other, Jericho indicating that we should extinguish our lamps. I followed his lead. In the darkness, I pressed my back against the wall of the cavern, trying to keep silent and stationary.

A lamplight began to approach, suffusing our chamber with a yellowish glow. The crunching of boots drew closer. I slowly slid my Bowie knife from its sheath and bent my knees, ready to spring at whoever was stalking us.

When the figure was within reach, I hurled my full weight against him, both of us landing on the rough floor of the mine. The lamp he'd been holding fell but didn't break. Jericho reignited his lamp, and I was able to look directly into the eyes of the skulking pursuer, my knife blade pressing against flesh.

Her hair was lovely, her eyes familiar and haunting. She smelled like soap and woman-sweat.

"Verbena," I said. "I almost decapitated you."

"I'm so glad you didn't," she said, patting her hair. "Would you please help me up?"

I grabbed her slender arm and pulled her to her feet.

Jericho failed to stifle a laugh. "Boss, we thought the ghost of Vestrick had appeared."

"I was worried," I said, "that Bad Jace was here to seal us inside."

"Sorry to disappoint, but I could use your help back at the Blood Nugget."

"Chaparral still unwell from his spill?" Jericho said.

"No, he's back at his piano. There's revolt brewing among the miners. John Mackay plans to hold a meeting at the church, and I'm sure it'll spiral out of control."

I noticed a thin line of blood on her neck. I retrieved a handkerchief from my coat and dabbed it. Her face was intrigued, her beautiful mouth slightly open.

Jericho cleared his throat. "I'll get the horses ready. See you both outside."

As he headed out, I used a match to reignite the wick of my lamp. Verbena went to leave, but I grabbed her arm.

"What were you really doing here," I said.

"What do you mean, Kid?"

"You're the one dragging all this crap into Vestrick's mine."

"I have no idea what you're talking about."

"You said, in the balloon, that you had something to tell me about the old Brit."

"I do."

"Tell me."

She yanked her arm from my grip. "Grinaker was trying to buy the rights."

"When."

"Before Vestrick died. Before he handed the claim over to you."

"Why would Grinaker buy a claim next to his abandoned stamp mill?"

"I don't know. But he dispatched a go-between, an ore-processing agent, to pressure Vestrick to make the sale."

Ore-processing agent. That was likely the man Vestrick had tussled with inside the Sure Cure, a fight I had to break up.

"I just can't figure out why the old Brit pushed this claim into my hands."

"He didn't want to sell it. He wanted you to have it, obviously."

"To do *what* with."

"Maybe there's another streak nearby." She turned to examine the walls of the pit. "Maybe there's a rich vein that he and Grinaker knew about."

"I'm not a miner. Vestrick, more than anyone, knew I'm more comfortable using a gun and my fists than I am picking up a shovel and wrecking my health with mercury."

"Smells like a bar in here," she said, making a face. "Urine and alcohol."

"Before you get too comfortable, we should leave. I'll check out Mackay's assembly."

"Obviously, I want the miners to get paid more. Their wages end up in my till. But Mackay cares for those men like they're his extended family. He knows they're flawed, yet he accepts them, nudges them toward a greater goal."

"Money," I said.

She shrugged. "Money is better than no money."

"Yes, but do you ever dream, Verbena," I said, "that there's a different way to live?"

"I don't dream. I count money."

"'A dream has power to poison sleep.' The poet Shelley wrote that somewhere."

"Sounds like something Vestrick would say."

"He was a fan of Shelley's verse."

Verbena touched my chest, looked into my eyes. "Do you feel poisoned, Kid? By your desires?"

"Poison is often an inoculation. At this point, I feel immune to everything, everyone."

"Even love?"

"Love," I said, "is a special kind of hell."

———

THE MINERS' meeting was held in First Presbyterian Church. Verbena, Jericho, and I stood in the very back of the prayer house. The three superintendents of the bigger operations on the Comstock Lode were there, with at least a hundred miners gathered. It was a bad sign, given that so many miners were motivated to reject the working conditions of absentee-owned mining corporations. Mackay was, of course, a boots-on-the-ground director of operations. He'd spent more time inside a hole in a mountain than all of his crew members combined. But the respect he earned meant nothing to the cutthroats and vandals who showed up to Virginia City based on flimsy, unrealistic newspaper ads in Texas, Oklahoma, and Arkansas. They'd seen it right there in print that jobs in Nevada were lucrative, and that the South would win the war lickety-split. They resented the misinformation they'd absorbed, which meant they rejected the wisdom and experience of men like Mackay.

Mackay was far from perfect, but he understood the experience of the working man and the outlook of the corporate master. He comprehended them both enough to believe that money could be generated to benefit everyone in Virginia City, as long as people stopped sabotaging others and themselves. He'd worked for four dollars a day as a miner and refused to pay his men anything less. The problem was that the US government was involved in a financial gambit to wage a war that couldn't be won, unless you counted fratricide as victory.

"If Governor Nye shows up to tour the mines, it means what we do for the war effort is important," said a dust-encrusted digger, who'd arrived at the meeting straight from Ophir. "If what we do is important, then that means we deserve six dollars a day!"

"We deserve *seven* dollars!" another miner yelled from the pews.

"Union!" shouted another.

The miners roared their approval, Mackay giving them time to vent their enthusiasm. Then he stepped forward to the lectern.

"My brothers in the mines," he intoned, "I believe that our efforts here are about more than making rich people wealthier. I believe that the work we do—honest, exhausting, and condemned by the daylighters—is helping to change the nation, pushing it toward a higher realm. What we do matters here and across the land for centuries to come. That said, we can't extort money at a time when our country needs us most. We have guests coming, and when guests arrive at our house, we don't argue, we don't bicker, we don't vandalize. No, we come together instead. We unite for the purpose of giving the men who led this country what they need in order to bring us out of political danger, to save us from the bloodshed of eternal war. The purpose of this visit by Nye is to inspire, to galvanize, to bind us together!"

"I heard that Nye is bringing President Lincoln!" a miner offered. "We don't want him here!"

"Speak for yourself, butternut," someone else scolded.

Suddenly a melee erupted, punches were thrown. Mackay raised his voice above the chaos.

"There's nothing in the papers about Lincoln coming here, as far as we know!"

Someone offered, "Newspapers are for wrapping fish, not reading!"

Again, the miners roared.

The scuffle receded. As Mackay tried to simmer boiling tensions, I noticed the dust-encrusted miner who spoke earlier wave over a large, dark-suited man with a gun on his belt from the chapel side of the church. He was brawny, awkward heavyweight and little stiff in his gait, but I could see that he knew how to move quickly, how to slap iron in a shootout.

Verbena noticed him too.

"Kid, do you know that guy?"

I shook my head.

"I suspect," Jericho leaned in to tell us, "Kid and that guy will meet very soon."

The dusty ringleader approached Mackay at the lectern, then turned to face the miners.

"We've been given excuses now for months," he said. "Even as silver stocks skyrocket, we're told to work harder, longer, faster. There's not going to be a visit from Nye, from Lincoln, from Jesus Christ—"

"This is a house of the Lord, you ingrate!" someone pointed out.

"Blasphemy!" a religious miner cried out.

"Until we get our six dollars, and now we have the muscle behind us to demand, not ask, for this wage increase before the end of this week.

"Who's the muscle? Your mama?"

There was loud laughter.

But the dust-bucket didn't back down. "No more hemming and hawing from the superintendents! Our man's name is Jester Trafton, and he's going to set everything right for us."

At that moment, the man in black stepped forward, thick-necked, wearing a hat inside a house of God. Poker-faced, he scanned the crowd like a steer in a Mexican bullfighting ring. I half expected him to paw the ground like a ready to charge.

Then this behemoth turned to Mackay and growled, "Meet me outside and bring your shootin' iron."

The church grew very silent. No creatures stirred, not even Sarah and her dogs, who now stood beside us in the vestibule.

The altar behind him, Mackay refused. "I'm not fighting a hired gun. But I'll send someone in my place to handle your hairless ape."

Nobody said anything. Nobody had to.

Everyone in the nave turned to see if the man was here, the man who'd fight Jester.

He was here.

I was the man.

Eventually, all eyes settled on me.

Jericho laughed, his voice echoing through the church.

"Told you these two were gonna meet soon."

21

MACKAY AND I DIDN'T SEE EYE TO EYE ON MANY issues affecting Virginia City. He was in the mining business to grow as wealthy as humanly possible. I was here to escape a brutal personal history and to avoid conscription in the Confederate army. Still, we shared the trauma of being raised in harsh environments that hardened us and, somehow, made us sensitive to the plight of others.

Born in Dublin, Ireland, Mackay's background was one of extreme deprivation, having grown up in a shanty, with dirt for a floor and a pig for a roommate. At age nine, he boarded a ship to New York City with his family. He ended up living for a time in a disease-ridden slum in lower Manhattan and hawking newspapers. At twenty, he took a clipper around Cape Horn to arrive in California, then made his way to Nevada, after hearing about the Comstock Lode, the first major discovery of silver ore in the US Mackay was King of the Small Claims, buying in bits and pieces, and profiting. He also served as superintendent for the biggest mining outfits, working hard to

process silver ore and to keep the miners from unioniz-
ing. He was well off, but we all knew something greater
lay in store for him. He was determined, destiny-bound.

He was also shrewd and curried favor with people he
needed. I was such a person. I was grateful for the times
he pulled my butt out of the fire for, say, killing a miner
who deserved killing, but who had friends that didn't
appreciate my continued presence in town. Mackay had
tipped me off to an attempt to have me lynched, giving
me time to neutralize the threat. He'd lent me money
when I needed it, and gave me work when it suited him,
paying me handsomely.

When challenged by Jester, Mackay looked to me
because we had an understanding. I owed him favors.
Now he was looking to collect.

I was happy to pay my debt now for two reasons.
First, I didn't like being beholden to someone. Second, I
took an instant dislike to Jester Trafton and wanted to rip
his arm from his socket and beat him to death with it.

Without a word to anyone, I headed to the center of
C street to wait for the duel to begin, Sarah and Typhon
trotting after me. Miners poured out of First Presbyterian, taking up positions along the boardwalk for
optimal viewing. Jester Trafton and the dusty miner
emerged, and if anyone had told Jester who I was, he
didn't seem worried. When he came out into the street
to meet me, he looked as calm and focused as a cobra
ready to strike.

"Sarah," I said. "You and Typhon can't stand here
with me."

"I followed Typhon," she said.

The dog started jumping on me and barking, as if he
didn't want me to participate in this ritual of death. I

didn't like Typhon's behavior, because it rattled my confidence. I knew I'd beat this guy in a draw, but there were plenty of things to go wrong in a gunfight. I didn't want to think that the goofy, three-legged mutt had any preternatural ability to see the immediate future.

"Well, move him over to the boardwalk. This is a lethal corridor now."

"Come on, Typhon," she said. The dog gave a soft whine and followed Sarah as she found a place to watch behind a hay wagon someone had left in front of the barbershop.

Jester and I squared off at a distance of twenty-five feet, within my yet-to-miss kill zone. I slowly pulled my coat back to reveal my Colt Army Model 1860 single-action revolver. He wasn't jacketed, and I could see that he carried a Smith & Wesson, a poor choice. The gun was underpowered, the handle flared, the chambering flawed. Jester wore a thick corduroy vest that didn't fit right and that I found distracting. He seemed to be recovering from an injury.

Whatever, I'd give him something from which he'd never recover.

I could sense the pregnant silence that typically preceded a gun duel was about to settle in, when the unthinkable happened.

Typhon changed his mind and came running out into the street, heading straight for Jester.

The man in black grinned acidly, turned toward the canine, and fanned the hammer of his pistol twice. Typhon yelped and went down hard in the dust.

"No!" Sarah screamed, running toward her fallen friend.

Jester raised his pistol again. For the last time.

I put three bullets into his chest, sparks flying, the metallic noise of bullets striking metal.

"What the hell?" a miner said, articulating the confusion we all felt.

Jester was on his back gasping for air, his gun in the dirt and out of reach.

I walked up to him and knelt beside him to inspect his vest. Beneath the holes, I saw a sheet-iron breastplate, the bullets I'd fired had flattened against the armor.

I punched him once, twice, in the face. He lay there dazed as I ripped away his corduroy vest and then the protective sheath, holding it up high in the air so everyone could confirm.

There was an audible gasp. No one had seen anything like it before.

Sarah held Typhon in her little arms, sobbing in grief. The poor creature was gone.

The monster was summoned now, and there was no controlling him.

I pointed my Colt at Jester, pulled the trigger, and sent him packing into the underworld.

"I have one more bullet!" I said, using a voice that wasn't my own.

Three miners dragged, kicking and screaming, their colleague who had challenged Mackay and hired the dead gunfighter who now festered in the street. I raised my pistol. They brought him forward, then released him while jumping clear of my gun sight.

"Kid, don't—"

I blasted the bastard off the ground and into the dust to where we all return. He groaned and died.

Sarah's tears wouldn't stop flowing. When I took

Typhon from her arms, her banshee screams were unsettling and yet entirely familiar to me. Her fists on my legs were like the patter of rain.

It was only funny in retrospect, but the miners removed their hats and gazed at the ground, sickened by what they'd just witnessed, what the actions of one of their own had caused a young girl to endure, had caused me to unleash.

Sarah followed me to Grover's, mewling the whole way, clacking her teeth in rage, her nose full of snot and dirt. When I presented the dog to my surrogate father, he didn't ask any questions. He stopped what he was doing to work on Typhon as I took long pulls from a whiskey bottle.

Finally, he placed the dog in a child's coffin full of desert marigolds and wheeled him out.

Together Sarah and I pushed Typhon's death barrow up to Boot Hill. Ezra was waiting for us. He'd already used a shovel to prepare a goodbye-hole for Sarah's beloved.

I didn't pray; Sarah could only sob. Ezra was catatonic from digging. Thank God for Poppy.

She showed up and recited a line from, I think, Psalms: *Precious in the eyes of the Lord is the death of his saints.*

———

THAT NEXT MORNING featured another farewell at Boot Hill. Vestrick's. It wasn't as heart-gouging as Typhon's farewell. The viewing at First Presbyterian was elegant and tasteful, with Ralston, Grinaker, and Samuel Clemens attending. Grover did a marvelous job with the presentation, and the flowers provided by Poppy's cousin Sing were on point—red roses, the national flower of

England. Chaparral played a proud yet moving rendition of "Crusader's Hymn: Fairest Lord Jesus" on the church piano that drew a tear to Verbena's eye. The sunshine-drenched funeral itself was solemn yet celebratory, and Poppy pronounced every word of "Ozymandias" correctly. People smiled at one another; there were many hugs. The gathering at the Blood Nugget afterward was festive; everyone seemed to want to share a humorous story about the old Brit, recalling his swaggering Anglo-bravado and his pretentious poetry. I refrained from drinking due to a slight hangover from all the whiskey I'd downed after Typhon's death.

Overall, though, I was in a better mood. After checking in with Sarah, who comforted herself with ginger ale, ice cream, and her other pooches at Ezra's shoeshine stand, I stopped into the bank. To my delight, my recent jobs, all lucrative, had gotten me closer to the nut I needed to buy an orchard. Mackay deposited a significant amount and left a note with the bank teller for me: "Thanks, Kid. Sorry about the dog. Yours, JM." An honorable man of few words.

I did the math in my head. If I pulled off this presidential security detail without getting myself killed, there was a great chance I could abscond from Virginia City before the next frost, with fall being the best time to start planting grapefruit trees.

I thought about sending a telegram to a California broker to arrange a deal. Then I recalled that I should assess Chaparral. He'd injured himself during the dogs-in-the-street fiasco, and I needed to confirm his fighting prowess for the Great Emancipator's arrival. Chaparral had played beautifully at the viewing, a good sign. He had a piano in his girlfriend Rosie's place, where he stayed. I knew he couldn't resist playing it, no matter how dizzy he felt. But hitting the keys and punching assassins are different activities. I was more interested in the latter at the moment.

When I knocked, Rosie answered. I heard Chaparral playing. She invited me in, embraced me.

"Kid," she said. "I'm so grateful. You retrieved my peepstone from that wicked Grinaker."

"Happy to help," I said. "You and I need to do a better job discouraging Chap from frequenting the Dead Dice. The house edge there is diamond-sharp."

"Poor Chap. He feels insecure because he's poor. He wanted to impress me with a big win."

"By losing your peepstone?"

Rosie shrugged, leading me into the kitchen. "I know he loves me."

"Well, you seem like a woman who's easy to love."

It didn't come out the way I wanted, but she didn't notice or care. "Chappy?"

The music stopped. "Yes, darling."

"Kid is here!"

I could hear the piano bench creak as he got up to greet me. He entered the kitchen and clasped me. "I haven't given you a proper thanks since your return."

"You gave me a big piece of information regarding Vestrick's claim. I'm grateful, Chap."

"Shucks, it was nothing. You know—"

I was already bringing my fist up to his temple when he performed a rear side high block and, lightning-quick, jabbed me in the chin, sending me crashing into the icebox and landing on the seat of my pants. I'd spent my childhood learning how to read a punch before it was thrown, but Chaparral could land shots that made me feel like a novice.

"Ouch," I groused, opening and closing my jaw, raising my arm so he'd pull me back to my feet.

He obliged. "I still got it, Kid."

"Yes, you do."

"Boys," Rosie scolded with a grin, taking my coat and hat and hanging them by the door. "If you're going to roughhouse, please take it outside."

There was no longer any need to test Chaparral's reflexes. He was a strange blend of natural boxer and formally trained composer. He'd grown up in San Francisco near a boxing gym, while his mother was a piano teacher who sought to make her son the next Stephen Foster. She let him box as long as he learned a new song every week. He related to me an amusing anecdote in which he, at age twelve, undertook a complete performance of "Camptown Races" while struggling to see the sheet music through two blackened eyes.

"The examination," I said to Rosie, "is complete. Your man is fit as a fiddle, an instrument he doesn't even play."

"He played your head like timpani," Rosie remarked with a snort, handing me a shot of whiskey.

"That he did."

"Chap," she went on. "Should we bring out the stone?"

"Oh yes!" he said. "Kid, Rosie wants to do a reading for you."

"She wants to see my future?"

"I've already seen it," Rosie said. "But we're closer to an event that looms so large in your life. More details might emerge this time."

"What do I need to do? Is it like the séances I've read about in *The Atlantic*?"

Chaparral closed the window curtains, darkening the room. "Even better."

Rosie lit a candle and pulled a cast-iron dutch oven pot from the shelves, placing it on the table.

"Better than what?" I said.

"You'll see," she said.

She used kitchen mitts to cradle the stone like a fragile potato before gently placing it in the pot.

22

ROSIE SAT AT THE TABLE, THE POT WITH THE stone inside it in front of her and took my hand and Chaparral's. She closed her eyes, and the room got very quiet.

Then she lowered her head, putting her face to the stone, but not quite touching it with her skin. There was a noise that I thought came from Rosie. Turned out it was just my stomach rumbling, since I hadn't eaten anything yet that day. I put aside my hunger pang so I could help her see clearly into the mystery of my fate.

"There's a presence here," she said finally, raising her head from the pot. Her eyes were white, as if she'd rolled them back into her head. Her face looked older yet somehow free of wrinkles.

I had to fight the instinct to pull my hand away. I glanced at Chaparral, who kept his peepers shut and seemed unfazed by what was happening.

"Who is it, Rosie?" he said.

"It's a terrible spirit. I see a man with a whip and a noose. He's drenched in the blood of his victims."

Although I didn't believe in hocus-pocus, it was obvious that she was referring to my father.

She inhaled suddenly, then spasmed her shoulders. "He's your relation. Yes, I think it's him."

"He's awful," Chaparral said, entranced by the ritual and privy to whatever vision his girlfriend was receiving. "Kid, how did you survive?"

I'd never told Chaparral or Rosie anything about my father, so his statement made the hair on my neck stand up. I wasn't mesmerized, but I was cold. Freezing. Rosie's hand felt like an icicle.

"What does he want?" Chaparral asked.

"He wants to warn Kid," Rosie said.

There was a droning sound, which I chalked up to the desert wind blowing outside. There was a buzzing, too, like the flies that had engulfed Dobie, the hydrogen-wagon middleman killed in Rattlepeak, Nevada.

"Rosie," Chaparral said, "I don't think Kid should hear any of this—"

"The man says there's a fierce battle coming that involves the Kid."

"I'm perpetually on the verge of battle," I said.

"In the sky. You'll be fighting in the sky."

I snorted.

"*Above* the mountain," Chaparral added. "The mountain is a gun."

"Chap," I said.

I could see his eyes moving beneath closed eyelids, but he didn't reply. He opened his mouth a little, caught in a dream state I wasn't sure I should interrupt.

"Your father insists there is an impostor in the desert," he said. "The impostor looks like a god of life, but he is the bringer of death."

Rosie's hand was ice-cold, burning my fingers.

"You must listen to him, Kid," she said.

I said nothing. The pain was really throbbing now.

"Beware of the mountain," Chaparral said.

I wanted to ask, *Which one?*

Suddenly, the dimmed lamp on the table came alive. Bright flame startled the three of us, ripping Rosie and Chaparral from their dream state.

I shook my hand to restore feeling, but the agonizing pain had vanished completely. I moved my fingers, and they were responsive.

Chaparral stood up, his chair scraping loudly against the hardwood floor. He took the lamp off the table and brought it to the sink to light a cigarette with it. Then he opened the curtains.

Rosie, her eyes back to normal, rubbed her temples, as if coping with a headache.

I stood up and reached for the whiskey that Rosie had poured me earlier. "Did you really see my father? Why was he invisible to me?"

"You don't have experience with the peepstone like Chap and I do."

My piano player nodded. "I had no idea."

"About what," I said.

"How badly you were treated." He picked tobacco from his lip, his hand shaking like he saw more than he could bear to explain.

I wasn't sure how much of this to believe. I wasn't so sure my father was dead. But I didn't tell them that.

"This wasn't a good idea," Chaparral said to Rosie.

"What do you mean?" she said. "He should know these things!"

I kept quiet, waiting for them to reveal more.

They were both momentarily silent, struggling to conjure the words.

"Whatever is arriving this week," Chaparral said, "is unlike anything you've encountered."

"Ghosts?" I said.

"Nothing supernatural. But it's definitely unusual."

What did that mean? And why would my father's spirit tell them?

"Tell him what we saw, Chap."

He covered his face with his hands. "We saw you jumping off Mount Ophir."

"How does that work?" I said.

"Your father," she said, "insists that you must do it. To win."

I couldn't believe what I was hearing. I laughed out loud.

"There must be a gas leak in here," I said finally.

Chaparral ignited the stove with his cigarette and put on some coffee.

"Is the impostor the bringer of death?" I said.

"Someone who's here in town, but under false pretenses."

Orion. But why? How?

"I take it back, Chap. You're not fit to join my security detail. I'll send Dr. Scullard over to diagnose you both."

"Kid," he said. "Let me be there with you. I've seen the vision. I might be able to help."

I picked up my coat and hat and headed for the door.

"One last thing, Kid," Rosie said. "Does the name Lilith mean anything?"

"No," I lied. I left Rosie's place and threw the door shut a little too hard.

I started thinking about Ophir. Was the mountain a weapon? Were people in danger of dying there? At Vestrick's memorial, I'd overheard Ralston sharing an idea to give President Lincoln a tour of the active mines.

Maybe Rosie's vision meant that someone was planning to shoot Honest Abe with a gun while he was on the mountain.

It was gibberish, except for one thing: I had to admit that Rosie and Chaparral knowing about my father's meanness and sharing the name Lilith suggested there might be something about the power of that weird Mormon rock.

Lilith was the name of the woman, a servant, who died shielding me from my father's wrath.

———

RALSTON AND ORION were enjoying grilled perch from Washoe Lake when I showed up at the Griddle of Doom. They were in a booth, the same one that Ralston and I had breakfasted in when he first shared the news of Lincoln's arrival and hired me on to run security.

I tipped my hat at Ralston, who indicated he'd see me at the bar when they were through dining. I ordered a warm root beer to settle my stomach from the tension brought on by the seer stone. Sitting on the bar was a copy of *Territorial Enterprise*, the newspaper that featured an article written by my recent acquaintance Samuel Clemens. It was a humorous, gleefully pointless description of Grinaker's new air-balloon ride. The piece wasn't actually bylined, however; in fact, it was presented as a letter from a fictional character named "Josh." Everything about the letter was sharp, irreverent, and good-naturedly eviscerating. It was way too smart and funny a piece of writing to appear in a frontier newspaper. I admired Mr. Clemens's writing, and if I was honest with myself, I wouldn't have minded reading more of it.

The Griddle of Doom bartender was a soft-headed,

soft-in-the-middle gent by the name of Flanagan who was always nosing into people's business instead of serving drinks. He'd seen me studying the newspaper and felt he should comment.

"*Territorial Enterprise* has a new writer," Flanagan said, "and I hear he's politically connected."

"All journalists are politically connected," I said. "That's how they cover politics and ensure they get a chance to parrot whatever information politicians think we should know."

Flanagan pondered this. "Now that you say it that way, I'm not sure what a paper that didn't cover politics would look like."

"Exactly."

He toweled a glass dry. "Did you hear about the miners' wives?"

"I know this joke, Flanagan."

"No, I mean what they're doing in preparation for the 'Big Event.' Governor Nye is coming to Virginia City, and I hear he's bringing President Lincoln."

"Why would Lincoln come to Nevada of all places?"

"This is an important territory for the Union. The federal government needs to buy our silver and gold bullion to support its currency and to mint coins."

"But why bring Lincoln *here*. How will he make the trek with all the railroad lines bombed?"

"They're not all bombed," Flanagan insisted.

"Maybe," I said, "he'll arrive by air balloon."

"I don't know about that. Grinaker has the only balloon in a thousand miles. And if you put Lincoln in a Dead Dice-branded balloon, Grinaker's likely to crash it, him being a sympathizer."

"Grinaker," I said, "seems to have a lot going on."

Suddenly, I felt Ralston's hand on my shoulder.

"Kid," he said. "That was a beautiful goodbye to Vestrick. Poppy recited the poem with grace and sensitivity."

"She did, indeed," I said, indicating that he and Orion should hop on stools and join me.

"Whiskey and beer?" Flanagan said.

They both nodded and pulled up to the bar, one on either side of me.

Ralston spoke first. "Couldn't have gone better, Kid. I've never seen a Union effort snuffed out so quickly."

"The dog did all the hard work," I said dryly.

Orion snorted, then thought better of it and downed his whiskey shot.

"Grover did a bang-up job on the pooch, and on the Vestrick funeral," Ralston continued.

"You paid for Vestrick's send-off, I understand."

Ralston stared off into his reflection in the mirror behind the bar. "Least I could do. He was one of the earliest. If he'd arrived a few days earlier, we'd all be working the Vestrick Lode."

I was tired of thinking about the past, so I said, "What's the plan with Mr. Lincoln? I need an itinerary, Orion."

He reached into his jacket for a slip of paper and slid it down the bar top.

I opened it and examined the schedule. Lunch at the Dead Dice with miners, show at the opera house, overnight stay in the Gold Hill, tour of Mount Ophir in the morning, and back on the train to San Francisco.

"Seems doable," I said. "Again, though, I have to ask, Where are the Pinkertons and US marshals, and how many?"

"Ten Pinks and five Marshals," Orion said. "They arrive with the President."

I mentally calculated. "That's a small security team. There are 4,000 people in Virginia City."

"Are all of them assassins?" Orion said, beer foam on his lip.

"No, but they'll be crowding the railroad station, the saloon, the hotel, and the opera house. And not everyone in town agrees with the Union on the issue of slavery."

Ralston jumped in. "That's where you come in, Kid. We need you to watch the ones who disagree with Lincoln's political stance."

"It's not a stance," I said, losing my temper. "It's the industrial half of the country slaughtering the agrarian half."

"Careful. I hear a bit of the grayback in you emerging."

He was only teasing, but his ongoing ignorance of what I saw and experienced in the South galled me.

"Ralston," I said, stepping off my stool. "You have no idea what you're talking about or who you're talking to. If you say something like that again, I'm going to whoop you butt-naked and hide your clothes."

"Stay calm, Kid," Orion pleaded. "We're all under a lot of pressure. Now look, if you consider your team—that's six more right there—plus myself, my brother Samuel, Ralston, and Mackay and his stridently pro-Union miners, that's an additional, what, fifty protectors in the crowd."

"I hope you're not giving them all guns."

"Kid," Ralston said. "Let me utter the words right now. I'm sorry I teased you. Now, here's what you need to know. Your team, the Pinkertons, and the US marshals have the weapons. Everyone else is a necessary pair of eyes, including Animal Girl and Ezra. It's all hands on deck. If someone spots danger or a threat, that's where you step in and nip it in the bud."

I hopped back on my stool, pounded my root beer, and slapped Ralston on the back. "I hear you, and will do everything in power to make this a smooth, incident-free visit for the Ancient One."

"Toast?" Orion said.

"Toast!" Ralston said.

Flanagan poured us each a shot of whiskey, which I planned to chase with my root beer.

I raised my glass and said, "Safety doesn't happen by accident."

"When safety is first," Orion said, "you last."

"Check yourself," Ralston said, "before you wreck yourself."

We all cracked up at this rhyme.

"When safety is first," Flanagan barged in enthusiastically, "you last."

We collectively gave him the stink-eye.

Ralston and Orion engaged in conversation, and I remembered something.

"Say, Flanagan," I whispered to him. "You mentioned the miners' wives earlier. They're doing something special in preparation?"

"Yeah," he said, keeping his voice low. "The Virginia City Miners' Wives' Cooking, Sewing, and Civilizing Club is cooking a big pot of miner's stew for Governor Nye and for, well, you know—the President. For their lunch at the Dead Dice."

"Miner's stew. What's in it?"

"Everything you don't wish to know about."

23

I'D LEFT THE GRIDDLE OF DOOM, HEADING TO Grover's for the evening to catch some sleep in my coffin and to read a few pages of Newman's *Iliad*, when I heard someone coming up behind me.

I pivot-turned with my gun ready and the hammer cocked.

"Kid," a voice said. "It's me, Sleath."

Sleath Haggin. He was an old-time miner who worked independently of the big companies, still pick-axing and panning on a claim he'd owned for years now. Like Vestrick and Henry Comstock, he was among the first to find silver in Nevada. He was a drinker, spending whatever he'd made from his mine on whiskey at the Dead Dice and the Blood Nugget. I'd thought to see him at Vestrick's funeral or at the memorial, but he'd kept a low profile. He wasn't close to Vestrick, but Haggin had a connection with the old Brit that couldn't be undone. They'd worked together on claims and swapped parcels and stakes over the last several years, sometimes at the Assay Office, but mostly at poker tables and saloons.

I holstered my gun. "Had me worried for a second, Sleath. Missed you at the funeral today."

He removed his hat with both hands so that I could see his face more clearly. He was trembling, like he was suffering from alcohol withdrawal.

"You okay?"

"Yeah, I'm good. Thought better of attending. I'm *persona non grata* with those types."

I recalled Sleath's paranoia over the notion that men like Ralston and Mackay sought to sabotage his mining rights. He was convinced that men in power coveted his claims and would use any means, legal or illegal, to snatch them. I'd never done a job for him, but I had, early last year, socked a rambunctious idiot who'd been riding poor Sleath all night at the Nugget for being unable to hold his shot glass steady. I didn't work for free, but sometimes I saw stuff that required hasty, violent correction.

"Someone bugging you tonight, Sleath?"

"No, Kid. I wonder if you have time tonight for me to show you something."

"What is it?"

"Up on Ophir. Vestrick's claim."

"Already been there. Someone dragged a lot of quick-silver into the tunnel."

"That's not all."

"Saw that, too. Grain alcohol, and what else, urine?"

"There's even more now. Let's take a peek, Kid. You should know what Vestrick handed you."

I considered the possibility that someone might've enlisted Sleath to lead me to Ophir for an ambush. Seemed very unlikely, and the nagging mercury puzzle needed solving. So I agreed.

We took his mule wagon up the road that led to

Vestrick's side of the mountain, which faced Virginia City, on a lower plateau from where Grinaker launched his balloon. The stars were bright in the night sky. I thought about the idea of people living on or near those shimmering pinpricks. Then I thought about what people from other solar systems might think of me and my knuckle-dragging occupation. Here I was being driven up a mountain to examine a hole that someone had dug into the earth to secure riches and wealth. The biggest hole was inside me, however, and it would never be filled, not even by God Himself. I wondered if launching a golden orchard in California would be enough to patch the pestilent wound that was my heart. If Poppy didn't leave with me, I might find another woman who would go, but what was the point? If I wasn't enough for my Flower, I wasn't enough for any woman, no matter who she was or what she did. Besides, what girl on earth could ever love a hollow man like Kid Crimson?

When we arrived, I could tell right away from examining the tracks, even by dim lamplight, that more items had been wheeled into the tunnel.

"I only seem to visit Vestrick's site in the nighttime," I said.

"It's not haunted," Sleath assured me.

I wasn't concerned about ghosts. I didn't want anyone sneaking up on me in the dark.

We went inside and I spotted several boxes marked Patent B.

"I've heard of this powder," I said. "Mackay mentioned it before I left for the hydrogen wagon."

"It's powerful blasting powder," said Sleath. "Little bit'll blow you to kingdom come."

"Ever mess with it?"

"No. Too much kick for an old man like me."

"Happen to see who brought it here?"

He spit tobacco juice into the shadows. "I didn't, but it's a strange combination of elements."

"Mackay picked up the blasting powder from the railroad station three weeks ago. Let's assume it's his. Why store it here in dead Vestrick's tunnel?"

Sleath noted, "Kid, Mackay's company is clear on the mountain's other side. He's got plenty of storage over there."

"I'll talk to him about it. Problem is that Lincoln arrives in a few days. Perhaps Mackay moved the powder up into the mountain so that there was no danger to Lincoln in town."

Sleath shrugged. "They're supposed to take Lincoln up this way is what I heard."

"True. It's a scratcher, but I feel like I'm getting closer to understanding everything."

"You know, Kid, it's your claim. You have every right to move this stuff out of here. Your girlfriend's people will do it for cheap."

My girlfriend's people. "Yes, but I want to keep monitoring this place until it all makes sense."

I handed Haggin a few coins for his trouble, and he bowed in appreciation.

"Thanks, Kid."

"Thank *you*, Sleath. Let me know if you receive any more information."

We turned around to leave the tunnel when suddenly, from behind us, an explosion of bats clipped our heads, making Sleath shout in alarm.

"You all right, old timer?"

"Never got used to them. They carry rabies."

"I've heard that."

"Bats. Rats. Bedbugs. Vermin are always a problem."

"Especially," I said, "the two-legged kind."

———

MY SECURITY TEAM, including Ezra and Sarah, met at the Griddle of Doom. I ordered everyone pancakes and black coffee. We were in good spirits, our nerves jangled by the arrival of such an important guest, and by the risk we ran of getting involved in a violent skirmish. There was no tension between Chaparral and me. He and I embraced before sitting down to breakfast and picked up our friendship like a blanket, wrapping ourselves in its warm comfort.

"I always have your back, Kid."

"I know. And I have yours."

Before the food arrived, Ezra poured a bed of syrup onto his plate, scooping it up with his fingers to eat. Sarah elbowed him to stop, then presented him with a metal spoon. He took it and resumed consuming syrup, causing a big laugh in the booth. Sarah smiled at him with fascination.

Finally, our pancakes arrived, my teammates digging in like famished wolves. I was about to take my first bite when I spotted Mackay enter the establishment no doubt to order his usual Irish coffee. He had a bodyguard with him, someone I didn't recognize, tall and scowling.

"Excuse me, everyone," I said. "Quick bit of business."

They didn't seem to notice or care as I got up from the booth.

"Good morning, Mr. Mackay," I said. "I got your message and your gift the other day."

His bodyguard stepped between with his hand up, his other on the butt of his iron.

"It's okay, Croy. This is the Kid, the young man I mentioned to you yesterday. He saved my life and staved off a ploy for unionization. Kid, this is Croy Maldonado."

Saying nothing and refusing to shake hands, Croy nodded and stepped back, allowing me access to Mackay. The bodyguard then tipped his hat to me with a wry smile and sipped his coffee.

I ignored him and addressed Mackay. "Last night I found something interesting in the claim Vestrick gave me before he died."

"What's that, Kid?"

"DuPont patent B blasting powder. I seem to recall you mentioning a shipment."

"I did, and it arrived. What's your point?"

"Are you storing it in my tunnel?"

He bristled at the suggestion. "Why would I put *my* blasting powder in *your* mine?"

"That's what I'm asking."

He sipped coffee, gave me a sidelong glance. "All my powder is accounted for and safely stored. I don't know who has put what where, but it appears you have someone misusing your property. There are two other outfits there on Mount Ophir. You might check with them."

"Huh," I said.

"That side of Ophir, facing Virginia City," he went on, "has always been useless. Mr. Vestrick squeezed every deposit, every nugget, from that part of the mountain. The tunnel is, however, closer to a few different active mines. Someone may be using your site as storage, believing it to be inert, abandoned."

"Well, it is."

Mackay laughed and placed his hand on my shoulder. "Kid, if you want me to remove the powder, I'm happy to do it. It's expensive material, and I could always use more."

"There's no worry. I'll take your advice and ask the other superintendents. And Mackay?"

"Yes, Kid?"

"We're even."

He smiled. "For the moment, yes. Seriously, let me know if I can help."

We shook hands, and Croy and I exchanged unfriendly looks.

When I got back to the table, my security team was marveling at Ezra. He'd ordered another stack of pancakes and was messily plowing through them. He was showing off at this point, no doubt proving his potential as a record-breaking competitive eater in the near future.

"Can you believe this guy?" Jericho said.

"Bottomless half-pint," Chaparral said.

The Niño brothers just laughed.

Sarah rested her head on her hand, intoxicated by her boyfriend's appetite.

"Polish those off," I said, "and let's head to the scrap-yard for some shooting drills."

Less than thirty minutes later, we were at John John's place, listening to the squeals and chicken clucks as we conducted our training. We focused on Ezra and Sarah giving us hand signals to confirm the location of a possible assassin. We divided the Virginia City downtown into five sections. A fist pushing down followed by five fingers displayed meant someone with a knife ready to draw in section five. An index finger and thumb pointing up followed by three fingers meant a gun-wielding assassin in section three, and so on. Two palms pressed up signaled that there was an assailant on the roof, and we worked out our sightlines in scrapyard, showing Ezra and Sarah how to work the environment for better vantages: stepping on a crate for an elevated angle or getting under a wagon to catch someone loading a rifle from a prone position.

"What if," Ezra said, smartly, "an assassin is in front of me, blocking me from signaling?"

Sarah quietly sneaked behind Jericho's legs and made a table with her body. Ezra took the hint and pushed the bartender over, causing him to fall over Sarah's impromptu tripping stance.

Ezra and Sarah darted away as Jericho chuckled, brushing the dust from his pants.

"Not bad," I said.

Then we spent time teaching Chaparral how to draw and to dry-fire his pistol. He was a phenomenal boxer, but his gunmanship was threadbare, so much so that I considered taking away his pistol. He was more likely to injure himself or a friendly than nullify a threat.

Poppy showed up late. We got her caught up on the hand signals and how to best position oneself during President Lincoln's arrival.

"Do you think you'll be able to confiscate everyone's guns before?" she said.

"Yes," I said. "If they want to stay in Virginia City that day, they'll need to comply."

"Even Bad Jace?"

"Well, that's different. He's one of us, at least for the time being."

"I'm anxious, Kid. Everything feels weird. Did you notice there's nothing in the newspaper about Lincoln? The journalist, Sam Clemens, only states that Governor Nye is en route."

"Maybe they don't want people from Carson City coming down and causing a ruckus."

"What if there's commotion? Kid, no offense, but this job seems too big for you and the Blood Nugget boys to handle by yourselves."

"We'll handle it. Or die trying." I thought about Rosie's peepstone prediction, which sounded to me like a suicide mission. I didn't want to die protecting the President, buy this was a once-in-a-lifetime job. And I didn't intend to depart this world quietly.

Poppy stepped forward to kiss my mouth. "That," she said, "is why I'm fearful."

24

WE SPENT THE NEXT DAY STRIPPING EVERY ONE
of their guns. We knew we couldn't possibly secure every
single weapon, but if we could get enough of them off
the streets and set a no-nonsense tone, the whole affair
would go smoothly, quickly. The rule was simple. You
were only allowed in Virginia City if you checked in your
firearms upon setting foot in town. A few ding-dongs
tried coming in from the foothills of Sun Mountain, but
John John's gunpowder-sniffing pigs headed them off,
squealing horrifically whenever they encountered a miner
packing iron. Then Sing and Butenhoff confronted the
miners and processed their guns before bringing them
back to Grover's, where they were cataloged and locked
inside unsold caskets.

Chaparral, Jericho, and I handled the main access
point leading from the mines. Miners tended to take
their guns with them on-site for fear of being robbed or
rousted. They gave us lip, but when we explained that
there was no chance that they'd be able to drink, gamble,
and womanize in peace, they relented. We used the

men's own vices as leverage. We also provided them a free drink ticket they could redeem at the Dead Dice or the Blood Nugget to soften their anguish. We created, in essence, the first gun-free city in the history of the West. We didn't do it to protect the residents, naturally. We did it to shield a president who'd plunged his nation into an apocalyptic conflict that showed no sign of ceasing.

There was one instance when things got tricky. A gaggle of miners that had skipped the morning caravan to Ophir and ended up drinking all day in the Dead Dice and then walking around town with iron on their belts. The miners whose guns we'd confiscated noticed, mistakenly believing that the armed miners had gotten free drinks, and began raising hell, and went so far as to start attacking the armed, highly inebriated, AWOL-from-work miners. It was one of the dumbest things I'd ever seen happen in Virginia City. Naturally, fistfights broke out, guns were drawn, and few people were killed as a result of gun-packing, alcoholic miners having skipped their shift. It was a typical frontier boondoggle.

In any case, Dr. Scullard was called in to treat the victims. He generated more havoc than he allayed, malpracticing on multiple patients, and even injecting cocaine instead of morphine into one poor soul whose ankle had been broken by a horse. The energized miner ended up running from Scullard's medical tent on foot, returning to the mine and back, because he'd left his wallet behind and he wanted to play a few rounds of blackjack due to how great he was feeling.

These issues aside, we collected nearly 1,000 guns from people in Virginia City. My bosses were impressed.

"Kid, I didn't think it could be done," Ralston said later at Blood Nugget. "Gunpowder sniffing pigs! How do we get you elected sheriff?"

"You've made things much safer for President Lincoln," Orion confirmed.

"Let's see how it all pans out before you swear me in," I said.

They nodded. Together we toasted, this time to the success of Lincoln's stopover.

After a moment, Ralston aroused my suspicion by mentioning that Bad Jace hadn't been seen lately, hadn't participated in the gun grab.

I shrugged. "Figured he was assisting Grinaker with balloon logistics."

Orion narrowed his eyes and looked at Ralston, who took another sip of whiskey.

Finally, he said, "It doesn't make financial sense for Grinaker to wreck his cash cow."

"His cash cow," I said, "meaning..."

"Meaning Virginia City," Orion explained.

"No doubt Grinaker has Confederate sympathies," Ralston continued. "But his strongest loyalty is to money."

"And there's lot of money to be had here," I said, "as long as the mines keep producing silver."

"I trust Grinaker about as far as he can count banknotes."

"Well, you must trust him infinitely, in that case. Because that guy adores wealth."

"Money is only worth what people believe it's worth," Orion qualified. "Inflation changes value, and changes minds."

"You think Grinaker will change his mind tomorrow?"

"No," Ralston said, "but I conducted a little research into his purchasing."

"Research, huh," I said. "He'd never show you his

ledger. You broke into Grinaker's office."

Orion pushed his tongue against his cheek, suggesting I was correct.

Ralston swatted away my remark as if it were a housefly. "He's buying blasting powder."

"Is he storing it in the tunnel that I inherited?"

"Oh, the claim Vestrick gave you. I heard something about that."

"Grinaker probably thinks the mine is forlorn. He's using it as storage, though I don't know why. He has plenty of other sites to keep that stuff."

"Have you asked him?"

"No, but I'm keeping a close eye on the place. Or rather Sleath Haggin is."

"Haggin. He's a strange one."

"Who's this?" Orion said.

"A grubstake miner going back several years," Ralston explained. "He knew Henry Comstock."

"He thinks there's something odd about the material being thrown in there."

"What's all there?"

"Again, the blasting powder. And I swear Grinaker's added grain alcohol and, well, urine."

Ralston harrumphed. "That's just the odor of Vestrick and Haggin spilling liquor and relieving themselves."

"Maybe."

Orion looked concerned. "Should we strike the balloon ride?"

"Balloon ride? What are you two talking... Oh no." I lowered my head, chin touching my chest.

Ralston had a big smile on his face. "You're not enthused, Kid?"

Even Orion was grinning now, which made no sense.

"Is this a joke? The President can't be on his way."

"I assure you," Orion said, "that Lincoln arrives tomorrow morning on the train."

"You can't put him in a balloon with a grayback partisan. Why do you protect him?"

"Lincoln won't be alone with Grinaker," Ralston clarified yet ignoring my question.

"That's somewhat better," I said. "You must send a Marshal with balloon-piloting experience."

"We're sending *you*, Kid."

Orion raised his glass in my honor.

I didn't reciprocate the gesture.

I was about to roll up my sleeves and start punching sense into their skulls when Jericho tapped my shoulder.

He leaned over the bar. "Something's up at the Sure Cure."

"Gentlemen," I said to Ralston and Orion. "I need to exit at this moment, but I'd love to rekindle this discussion later tonight."

"We're here," Ralston said, "if you need us."

I left my drink untouched at the bar.

———

INSIDE THE SURE CURE, I was expecting to remedy a situation involving an opium partaker and Poppy, most likely over payment issues. Sometimes, in an utter stupor, men would attempt to smoke or ingest more than what they paid for, occasionally even grabbing other customer's goric. This resulted in fights that Poppy didn't feel comfortable quelling. This is why she summoned me to her establishment, day or night. I was always ready to help.

What I never expected to encounter was the sight of my beloved Poppy in a straight-up knife fight with the owner of the Blood Nugget, Verbena, inside the Sure Cure, with stewed customers in their beds calmly observing the mayhem.

I wasn't stupid enough to jump between them and break it up. I needed to get behind one or the other and put her into a full nelson. The way they were positioned, however, with puffers crammed into the space, made it difficult for me to approach their blind spots.

"Kid," Poppy growled, "if you try to stop me, I'll carve you up too."

"Stay out of this, Kid," Verbena verified, voice rough with anger.

"I'm not letting you two hurt each other," I said, but as I lunged, I stupidly smashed my cranium against a low-hanging chandelier. I had to concentrate to prevent losing consciousness. I touched my forehead to make sure I wasn't bleeding.

Meanwhile, Verbena lunged with her blade, a steak knife she'd obviously brought with her from the Blood Nugget. Poppy turned sideways, dodging the attack, but with her knife hand behind her she was forced to use her bare fist to rap Verbena on the nose, sending her backpedaling.

Because there was an opium bed on the floor, Verbena fell down and into a prone position. Poppy went flying, knife coming down to land in the saloon owner's heart. But Verbena was no slouch and grabbed a nearby pillow for the block, Poppy's blade ripping into and across the fabric and sending goose feathers flying into the air.

Verbena kicked my girlfriend's ankle, bringing her to the ground, then rolled into a standing defensive posture. Seeing that Poppy had knocked her elbow against a lamp and lost her blade—a small, fruit-peeling knife that Poppy used when she felt peckish—Verbena pressed her attack with a wild, full-swing slash that narrowly missed Poppy's pretty face.

Feathers in her hair and on her feet again, my girlfriend gripped the unshattered lamp glass in both hands, smashing it against Verbena's shoulder. There was a crashing noise from the impact, but it didn't deter her from push-kicking Poppy in the stomach. The saloon owner charged, nearly getting her face walloped by a small shovel that I'd assumed Poppy had mounted on the wall for decoration.

It was decorative, but also a real shovel. Poppy threw it at Verbena, who ducked in time. She hiked her skirt so that her legs could pump easier, then ran full-tilt at poor Poppy, knocking them both over a sofa and onto the floor. They screamed in anger, in frustration at not being able to quickly kill the other, pulling each other's hair.

"Kid," Sing said, confused by my hesitation. "Feel free to break it up, okay?"

Stunned from banging my head and exhausted from confiscating people's guns and working on zero hours of sleep, I'd been hypnotized while watching my girlfriend in fierce combat with another woman. Shaking off my trance, I went to help Poppy to her feet. Instead of taking my hand, she cuffed my naughty bits, causing me to see spots and to lose my balance. I fell into the lap of a chandoo-smoker, who didn't seem the least bit troubled, bringing the pipe stem to my mouth. Groaning in pain, I pushed it away and rolled onto my side and adopted the fetal position.

"Kid, oh no!" Poppy said. "I'm so sorry."

"Is he okay?" Verbena asked, pulling her long, blonde hair from her sweaty face.

"I'm—I'm—" I was unable to finish, much less launch, my sentence. For reasons I couldn't fathom, the tension between the two women dissolved after I'd gotten hurt.

"I didn't mean to hit you there," Poppy continued. "I know it's so sensitive in that area for boys."

"For *men*," I sobbed, my voice an octave higher. "I'm a man!"

"A warm bath will make him feel better," Verbena said. "I'll go prepare one."

"There's a basin in the backroom," Poppy said. "The stove is right to next it. I'll get him ready."

As Verbena prepared my bath, Poppy gently stripped me down, carefully removing each article of clothing. "Do you need ice, baby...you know, in that area?"

"Don't freeze them," I said, still smarting. "Please."

She brought me a fresh robe and watched me struggle to slip it on and tie a knot in the front. She reached forward to help me, and I flinched, unsurprising given that she'd hurt me moments ago.

"Why were you two fighting?" I asked.

"It wasn't over you, silly," Poppy said, laughing.

"Why then?"

"She accused me of using her credit line at Roscoe's House of Hammers."

"Did you?"

She brought her hand to her chest, mouth agape. "Of course not. But someone representing me went in there and walked off with a whole bunch of grain alcohol, metal nuts, mercury, ball bearings, and gunpowder."

"Some of that sounds familiar."

"I want to get to the bottom of it, but she made me angry. So we fought."

"How did she anger you?"

"She said the only reason Roscoe gave the person all that stuff is because I'm your girlfriend. People know better than to deny you things, and I reap all the benefits."

"So it *was* about me."

She shrugged. "The way she said it made her sound like a bi... Like a not-nice person."

"His bath is ready and bubbly!" Verbena said from the back.

Poppy led me, hobbling yet slowly recovering, over to the bathtub.

Then I was bathed and pampered by two of the most beautiful women in the West. I watched them remove their clothes and tend to each other's dings and cuts, Poppy dabbing Verbena's bare shoulder with iodine and Verbena applying a cold compress to the welt on Poppy's navel.

"I'm sorry I went a little crazy on you," Verbena said.

"I'm sorry, too," Poppy said. "Friends?"

They kissed each other on the lips and giggled deliciously. They kissed again. Then they went back to sponging my neck and back.

I couldn't enjoy it. I had to get cleaned up and ask Roscoe who had taken all those materials.

25

I DROPPED IN ON HOUSE OF HAMMERS, BUT THE hardware store was closed on account of Lincoln's impending visit. I had no idea where Roscoe lived or if he stayed in an apartment above the store. Everything was locked, dark, and I had to remind myself that Roscoe sold more guns than hammers. It was a good thing he'd closed up shop early. Indeed, it was likely that Ralston or Mackay or both had urged him to stop selling firearms in the overture to the big event.

Still, it would be helpful to know who had acquired the items charged to Verbena, materials that seemed to be popping up inside the mine Vestrick had bequeathed me. It had to remain a nagging mystery, I guessed, until the President was on his way back to Washington, DC. Though I wished I'd taken my time and enjoyed the warm, soapy bath provided to me by both Poppy and Verbena who, just minutes prior to scrubbing me clean, had been trying to knife each other.

I had brought out, perhaps intentionally, petty jealousy and maternal competition in the two women. I didn't pretend to understand the so-called fairer sex, but I had a decent idea what made women happy—attention and generosity. Things my mother yearned for and never received from my father. Things I did my best to give her in the short time that I knew her.

I was only nine years old when she died. I recall spending time with her in the parlor, playing chess with her, piecing together jigsaw-puzzle paintings of Scottish castles, drinking her sweet iced tea with lemon. I hung on her every word, as she did mine. I told her stories of knights and horses, while she dazzled me with tales of indentured princesses and the saga of Joan of Arc's ferocious faith. My mother babied me; I loved her for it. When she died, she stranded me in a hellscape with a monster obsessed with inflicting pain on others, especially the vulnerable and powerless, before killing them slowly. He'd tried to kill me, but it didn't work.

In the end, the monster inside me was more terrifying than the one inside him.

My mother's death scarred me. Yet what frightened me more than my father's destruction of her was watching his behavior play out on an institutional level. Slavery. Politics. War. The desire to wield power in order to torment others was a human sickness that couldn't be cured by God or laws. The illness struck everyone, particularly those who believed themselves morally superior. John Brown the abolitionist, was the best example of humanity's incontinent predilection toward violence in the name of morality and societal regulation. In his effort to thwart slavers and liberate slaves, Brown killed a black railroad worker, something I'd contemplated at the war's outbreak. I had the choice to either fight for the South, alongside bastards who couldn't afford a single slave in a hundred years, or to enlist with the Union, fighting alongside Irish immigrants who couldn't afford to buy their way out of conscription. War was madness and the reason I fantasized about a grapefruit orchard far away from men and their lust for power and death.

I had more respect for men who drank their lives away in Virginia City. Men like Sleath Haggin, who was, at the moment, wobble-walking down C Street with a bottle in his hand.

"Sleath," I said. "Know where I might find Roscoe at this hour?"

"I'll take you right to him," Haggin hiccuped. "Follow my shadow, young warrior."

We made our way through an alley that led to a barrel fire behind the Dead Dice. There Roscoe was, drinking whiskey, his eyes fire-bright, his face rendered by flickering shadows. He seemed inebriated, or exhausted from the effort of running a store in a boomtown at the edge of America. As I approached him, I sensed Sleath peeling away.

"Hello, Roscoe," I said.

"Kid," he said. "Surprised to see you here."

"I'm surprised too."

"Bad Jace is back to smelling pretty ripe again."

"Well, he doesn't trust the science of soap."

"He did give me quite a few drink tickets, though." Roscoe raised a bottle with a smile.

"Bad Jace was in your store recently?"

Roscoe gave a bemused look. "Earlier today, on behalf of you and Miss Poppy. He said Verbena was covering the cost."

"What did he end up walking away with?"

"A lot of things. Mostly ball bearings and gunpowder."

"Anything else?"

"Arsenic. Lots of it."

"Did he say where he was taking it the arsenic?"

"I noticed him driving over to the Dead Dice immediately after," Roscoe said nervously. "Say, Kid, I assumed you and Bad Jace were partners now, after the Grinaker job. Need me to take all the stuff back from him? I won't charge Verbena."

I shook my head. "What about the rest of the stuff?"

"He was wheeling it up Mount Ophir."

"Thanks, Roscoe."

———

THE NEXT MORNING, Virginia City buzzed with anticipation as word spread that President Abraham Lincoln was making a historic appearance. The women of Virginia City had draped the streets in patriotic bunting, promoting a spirit of unity as we all eagerly awaited the Ancient One's arrival.

Lincoln's train pulled into our little station, and people gathered along the streets, reverence and curiosity in their features. Chaparral, Jericho, and the Niño brothers kept everyone off the railroad platform, where Orion, his brother Samuel, Ralston, Mackay, Grinaker, and I waited to receive the President. Grover was with us, too, accordion camera mounted on a tripod.

"Can you believe this is happening?" Grover said.

"I can't," I said.

"Seems like a dream."

"Hopefully it doesn't turn into a nightmare."

The locomotive clattered to a halt, brakes screeching, releasing steam with a prehistoric groan. The Pinkertons and US Marshals, all of them fierce-looking and strapping young men, stepped off the train first. They scanned us and everyone else for threats. Wielding shotguns and rifles, they moved quickly, taking up positions and exuding an aura of vigilance.

Eventually, a tall, lanky figure emerged, clad in a distinctive black suit that emphasized his somber demeanor. Lincoln's iconic stovepipe hat cast a shadow over his weathered face, marked by deep lines that reflected the weight of the nation's turmoil, and perhaps his own fury at having had to engage in a war that might very well tear the nation asunder and drown it in blood. There were many cheers and no booing, though not everyone was obviously thrilled by his presence.

Orion introduced each of us to Lincoln, who said nothing. His eyes were sad and intriguing, but his mouth was immobile. It dawned on me that he was saving his voice in preparation for a speech he was about to deliver in Virginia City. He kept his physical movements to a minimum. He was clearly someone who didn't believe in wasted words or actions, an aesthetic I approved of but couldn't adopt for myself. I wasted everything, starting with my life.

Orion arranged for a photograph to be snapped by Grover. The Marshals patted down each of us before letting us gather around Lincoln for a group portrait. Grover gave us a countdown, and we lifted our chins to present ourselves as dignified, stately, worthy of being in the same image as the President. Somehow, I ended up standing directly next to Lincoln. He smelled like stale wool and wood smoke, which indicated to me he wasn't at all a sensualist. Lincoln appeared, to me anyway, to be a man devoid of pleasure.

Grover, excited to have snapped a photo of me next to Lincoln, pulled his head from out of the camera's black-fabric curtain, and smiled at me. I returned the gesture.

If Grover was happy, so was I. Though we both had mixed feelings about the war, we basked in the energized atmosphere of Virginia City, which we had never seen exude such fervor for anything other than money and alcohol and flesh.

Lincoln and his retinue of bodyguards made their way down the main thoroughfare as he waved to people applauding and shouting with admiration. I'd assumed that he would speak in front of one of the more symbolic structures like the Wells Fargo bank or even the *Territorial Enterprise* newspaper office. For whatever reason, he ended up stopping in front of the new opera house, where a small band of local musicians was waiting for him. The tuba, flatulating its low, raspy notes, was joined by a trumpet and trombone. The song was "John Brown's Body," a marching tune about the notorious abolitionist popular in the Union states during the war.

The music continued through the second verse, before Orion stepped in, bringing it to a sudden finish. He walked to the top of the opera house stairs and welcomed everyone, thanking local businesses for making the President's visit possible. He introduced Lincoln as a man of destiny, a man chosen by God to liberate the slaves and to inevitably unite the ruinous fault line that had erupted between North and South. Soon, the nation would be made whole again.

Although Orion wasn't a gifted speaker, the exhilarated crowd whooped and hooted. People were electrified to be in the vicinity of someone that destiny had chosen, someone epic and history-making. There was no doubt, in my mind or anyone else's, that Lincoln would change, not just the United States, but also the lives of nearly everyone on earth. Ours was a nation of profound fate, everyone watching us, learning from us, idolizing us.

Lincoln, known for his eloquence, didn't disappoint. Standing proudly if sorrowfully on the steps of the opera house, he delivered a poignant address. He evoked the principles of liberty and equality that the Founding Fathers had championed. The audience—mostly miners' wives and soft-handed men who didn't work in the mines —hung on every word. When he spoke of a "new birth of freedom," you could witness the power of his speech on the people listening, how it echoed through their hearts, a rallying cry for a nation intent on ripping itself into gory pieces to save the most vulnerable from the shackles of human cruelty. His words were, I'd later learn, a rough draft of what would become the Gettysburg Address.

There was a massive hurrah at the end of his speech, the crowd surging forward, people wanting an opportunity to shake the hand of the Great Liberator. The Pinkertons and Marshals were more than enough, however, to keep the crowd at bay. Everyone on my team was examining spectators in the crowd, searching for something unusual, hostile. Now and then, I'd make eye contact with Ezra and Sarah, but they had nothing to report, no hand signals. They were having the time of their lives, tasked with a big, important assignment like this, inspecting grown-ups for weapons and suspicious behavior. I couldn't help but smile at their zeal. Everything was going smoothly.

As Lincoln concluded his remarks and Orion began speaking again, Samuel Clemens and I were already entering the kitchen of the Dead Dice Saloon. Thanks to a tip from Flanagan, the Griddle of Doom bartender, I knew of the plot to poison the giant pots of miner's stew in an audacious assassination attempt on Lincoln. Rats were a problem in every mining town, and arsenic was used throughout Virginia City, from the blacksmith to House of Hammers to the Gold Hill Hotel. Arsenic was routinely and liberally applied in the nooks and crannies of kitchens, where food debris and crumbs and sticky areas were abundant. The difference here is that Bad Jace had brought over 100 pounds of the chemical element, which set off my alarm bells.

The ladies of the Virginia City Miners' Wives' Cooking, Sewing, and Civilizing Club seemed nervous when Sam and I set foot in their cooking area. Our town had long served as a gathering point for Confederate sympathizers. The Confederate army had even conducted recruiting efforts here several months ago in the dead of winter, even after Lincoln had dispatched dragoons out of Fort Churchill to disarm, arrest, imprison, and, in some cases, execute secessionists. Many miners, too, had made their way west for the same reason I did—to avoid conscription and make money. Still, resentment toward the North was palpable. Dumping arsenic in a stew intended for Lincoln and his contingent wasn't beyond the pale. Which is why, earlier this morning, I'd stacked the arsenic in the corner of the locked dry-goods storage closet.

Butenhoff was trying to snap the lock with a crowbar until he felt our eyes on him. He stopped what he was doing and squared up, gripping the iron tool so tightly that his knuckles whitened.

"You know, Kid," Sam said in the presence of Butenhoff. "The only way to keep your health is to eat what you don't want, drink what you don't like, and do what you'd rather not."

"Sure, but how do you feel about arsenic?" I said, staring with contempt at Butenhoff.

"My least favorite seasoning, but when sprinkled on vermin, it has a hygienic effect."

"You two are a funny couple," Butenhoff snarled.

"Against the assault of laughter," Sam said, "nothing can stand. Not even your elephantine frame, sir."

"Pencil-neck, did you just call me—"

"Yes, he did," I said. "An elephant."

Butenhoff growled, rearing his arm to smash Sam with the crowbar. But I'd grabbed a giant metal grater from the countertop to block the strike, the impact causing sparks to shoot.

He went to stomp on my foot. I'd seen him use that trick too many times in the Dead Dice. When he put his weight forward, I'd already pivoted with the shredder. He did his best to dodge the arc of my swing, but he wasn't fast enough, the raised cutting edges obliterating his nose, blood gushing everywhere and spattering the kitchen walls.

Sam picked up a pot of boiling-hot stew and splashed it on Butenhoff, mouth open in agony. He tried to scream, but the blistering liquid burned his vocal cords, rendering them useless. Then I smashed him unconscious with a heavy iron skillet.

The members of Virginia City Miners' Wives' Cooking, Sewing, and Civilizing Club went running toward the kitchen exit. Standing in their way was my favorite bartender, Jericho, finger pressed to his lips, with a gun raised in his other hand, insisting that they not scream.

"Ladies, I want you to stay calm and sensible," he said. "We're now going to prepare a splendid lunch for President Lincoln and his delegation. I hope the bread is fresh. Miner's stew tastes so much better when there's a still-warm loaf on the table."

A few of the women nodded, eyes wide with fear.

Soon they hustled to cart out the unpoisoned pots of stew into the Dead Dice dining room, where the tables were set up mess hall-style, with more than a few thirty-four-star flags on display. The children of miners had bathed that morning and were already seated, ready to lunch with the important collection of political leaders in the town's history. Chaparral had invited the kids to keep their mothers from poisoning the meal.

Followed by the brass trio, which busily played a well-known Union song called "Battle Cry of Freedom," Lincoln and his security team stepped into the Dead Dice, onlookers cheering him as he selected a place for himself next to a young girl and boy, shaking their hands. The two appeared happy if aghast that such an important person had deemed them suitable tablemates. They smiled, bringing their hands to their faces to obscure their laughter, and then covering their ears at and winced from the noise that the brass-blasting musicians generated. I must say that Lincoln seemed relaxed and to be enjoying himself immensely, while Governor Nye, in marked contrast, looked to be staving off a bout of loose bowels.

Eventually the Dead Dice tables filled with Lincoln's men, along with mining superintendents and dozens of their best workers, everyone smiling, chatting, happy to be sitting down to lunch in a saloon in the middle of the day rather than toiling in a hole. Soon, lunch was on. The President slurped his stew without anyone on his staff taste-testing it for poison. It seemed to dawn on one of the Pinks that someone should've conducted a food inspection. Once Lincoln ripped into a piece of bread, however, the agent shrugged and dug into his bowl.

I'd read somewhere that Lincoln didn't care for cariogenic foods like bread and pasta. I guessed you can't believe everything you read in the newspapers.

After the food was eaten, Lincoln stood up from his table and in a loud, clear voice thanked the Virginia City Miners' Wives' Cooking, Sewing, and Civilizing Club for preparing a delicious meal. He thanked them, too, for supporting their husbands in their efforts to mine the silver in Nevada, which the government needed to acquire to finance the war. Nevada miners were, he insisted, the ultimate American patriots of the West. The women, chastened from having been stymied in their plot to kill the President with arsenic, stared at the ground and didn't make eye contact with the man who many of them wanted dead.

I didn't mention the poison plot to Ralston and Orion. If Grinaker was involved, I needed to be sure. After all, I couldn't just kill one of the most important men in Virginia City unless I was sure that he was a conspirator. Ralston and Orion didn't want me to take him out.

Why exactly that was, I couldn't figure out.

26

THE OPERA HOUSE IN VIRGINIA CITY HAD nothing scheduled during the week of the President's visit. Traveling singers and production crews didn't enjoy the heat of a sweltering western desert summer. There had been talk at one point of bringing in English soprano Louisa Pyne, but lingering arthritis had kept her from touring the States in June. Entertainment, therefore, happened to fall into the lap of my favorite musician and boxer, Chaparral. When he received news from Samuel Clemens in the Blood Nugget, where we'd been drinking after the successful lunch at the Dead Dice, that he'd been tapped to perform a piano recital for Lincoln, my good friend stood on his hands, balanced his legs in the air for a spell, and rodeo-hollered.

"Kid," he said, grabbing me by my shoulders, eyes wild with excitement. "What songs should I play for Uncle Abe?"

"Let me suggest," I said, "that you only perform songs you know well."

Giddy with excitement, he leaned back and squawk-howled like a demonic rooster, shaking his fists. "This recital will launch my career! I'll be working on Broadway before the year's done!"

"I sure hope so," Verbena said with a grin. "I don't know if I can stomach listening to you play 'The Old Gray Mare' one more time without puking."

"That tune is what we call in the business *a crowd pleaser*." Chaparral laughed. "Sam, you have to write me up in the *Enterprise!*"

"Oh, I most certainly will," Clemens said. "I've yet to set foot inside the opera house, an unexpected marvel, rising as it does against the rugged landscape. An oasis of refinement amid the frontier chaos, standing proudly and in marked contrast to the wooden shanties around it."

"He's already writing the article," I noted.

"Sam hasn't heard me play yet!" Chaparral said.

Ultimately, the young music-maker dazzled onstage, in front of the most important man in the United States. Chaparral raced through a medley of saloon favorites, goosing each song with classical flourishes and allusions that made those familiar with refined music chuckle. Chaparral even blended a bit of Bach into popular tunes like "Oh! Susanna" and "Old Black Joe." He moved into a segment of romantic pieces by Beethoven, "Für Elise" and Chopin "Études," culminating with his original composition, "Eternal Progression, for Rosie." It was bittersweet, languorous, every bit as wonderful as the material he played before it. I had to admit that he looked amazing up there—confident, debonair, other-worldly, framed by heavy velvet curtains. The echo of his piano resonated through the hall, filling the space with lush melodies that temporarily silenced the clamor of the outside world.

Throughout the free, open-to-everyone recital, Samuel Clemens, under dim, flickering gaslights, wrote in his reporter's notebook, no doubt preparing an account of the evening. The President, meanwhile, kept his head bowed for most of the performance, which I misinterpreted as him having fallen asleep. Instead, I saw that he was moved by what he heard, baggy eyes moist with emotion. My initial read of him lacking sensuality and aesthetics seemed wrong. The other attendees, miners and shopkeepers and bankers of Virginia City, had donned their finest attire. The scent of cigars mingled with the perfume of well-dressed ladies as they eagerly anticipated the next song, enthralled by the virtuosity of the local boy and saloon piano-banger.

The performance lasted for an hour, and then Orion was once again speaking to everyone. As Lincoln left the theater with his contingent, the Secretary of Nevada relayed that, in the morning, Lincoln planned to tour the mining operations at Ophir. The road to the mines would be blockaded. Workers were required to meet their superintendents at the base of the Ophir in order to gain access to their sites. Upon hearing this no one complained, people seemingly realizing that, for tomorrow at least, security would be tight given our visitor.

With the President safely ensconced in the Gold Hill Hotel along with his security team, I stalked the perimeter. I watched for strange antics, for gunpowder bombs, for lone figures lurking in shadows near the building. Aside from the bustling saloons, it was a placid night, the day's activities having exhausted Virginia City residents, pushing them into their beds so they might be rested to see Lincoln back on the train and returning to Washington, DC I was tired, too, but also galvanized by witnessing the sway that Lincoln's visit had on our town. I'd never seen my friends smile so much, look so pleased, enjoy so much success.

Grover beamed from his photographic work, Chaparral basked in the musical spotlight, Poppy and Verbena embraced the customers thronging their establishments, Jericho made enough in tips in a single day to put money down on a real house, the Niño brothers sent and received hundreds of telegrams through their office, and Ezra and Sarah shined shoes until their fingers ached. It wasn't money that brightened their lives, though it helped. The presence of, and recognition from, someone of historic consequence elevated their spirits. Lincoln was a divisive figure, true, but even secret bushwhackers felt monumental grace emanating from Lincoln. They saw vivid possibilities in a dark, corrupt world, even if for one day in this desolate, depraved boomtown. To my surprise, I watched whites treat Chinese immigrants and Paiutes with marginally greater respect, as more people from every social stratum began appearing in the streets, hoping to catch a glimpse of the Great Emancipator. When he reached out to touch the lives of these people, shaking their hands or sharing words with those who eked out an existence on the margins of Virginia City, everyone observing it seemed flabbergasted, invigorated.

After being relieved from my security shift by Jericho, I couldn't sleep due to all the excitement. I ended up drinking root beer in the thronged Blood Nugget, where Verbena was tending bar herself. Apparently, Ralston, Mackay, and Croy Maldonado had found no efficacy in counting sheep either. They ordered whiskeys, and we took our drinks over to a table and plotted out the morning's events. I tried to avoid eye contact with Cory for fear of getting angry enough to punch him in the throat. He was mixed race, like myself, but I sensed no brotherhood in him. He was just another cutthroat set loose in the Nevada wilderness to make money and hurt people.

"Grinaker's taking the balloon up to the top of Ophir Peak," Ralston said. "We'd like you to be there with Lincoln to meet him." He looked at his watch. "That's in a few hours, I guess."

"I'll be there," I said.

"I don't know if it's the same for you," Mackay said, "but Virginia City feels entirely different."

"The atmosphere," I said, "is remarkably improved. Can we keep him?"

Ralston laughed. "A good performance has that effect. Chaparral did his part too."

The notion that Lincoln performed a role bugged me, but I let it go. "Chap is the best saloon musician in the West. He's destined to play better venues than a Nevada opera house."

Croy Maldonado seemed to smile too much and too long at this.

"Mackay, where did you find your bodyguard?" I said. "Something is off about him."

Everyone at the table went tense, except for Croy and myself.

"Coming from the root beer boy," he said, standing up, hand on his iron.

Then I got up.

"You two are deader than cans of corned beef, so please, both of you, take your seats," Ralston said, paternal anger and weariness in his voice. "We're all tired and on edge from yesterday's events, and we're eager for tomorrow to go off without a hitch."

"Croy, come on," Mackay said.

Grinning, the bodyguard sat down again, his malevolent smile replaced with a snarled lip.

The scene was starting to bore me.

"I should get going now if you want me on top of Ophir Peak before dawn," I said.

"Find Bad Jace yet?" Ralston asked.

"No, but when I do, I'll let you know."

"If he doesn't find you first."

"I'm ready for that possibility."

"I'm sure you are," Ralston said.

As soon as I left the Nugget and stepped into the night air, Jericho came running up.

"Why'd you leave your post?" I said.

"Well, it's Sarah," he said.

"What about her."

"She says Ezra has been missing since Chaparral's concert."

"Did anyone check with Poppy?"

"That's where Sarah went first. Poppy brought her to me. We already checked Grover's."

"Let's not overreact," I said. "He might be tracking someone suspicious. He fancies himself a dime-novel detective."

Jericho nodded. "Gold Hill is graveyard-quiet. I'll head back there now."

SLEATH HAGGIN WAS available to take me up the mountain on his mule cart. On the way, he nipped from a bottle, chatting about the many changes he'd seen in Virginia City, how it had sprouted overnight after he and Henry Comstock struck the Comstock Lode. The town was named after another miner with the nickname of

Old Virginny Finney, who had passed out in front of the first saloon that had opened for business, which Grinaker bought out a year ago. Sleath had no idea what had happened to either Comstock or Finney, though he expected the former had returned to his previous occupation of fur trapping after selling his initial, barely profitable claim.

"To think," he said, "that this place now pays for the bullets and bombs for one side of a war. It really is incredible. To think the *President* came here!"

"I confess," I said, "that I didn't imagine this place being so crucial to the Union."

"Ugly places are often more important than they look."

"Ugly people too."

Sleath took a sip of whiskey. "Honest Abe honestly has a burnt boot for a face."

"Some women find him unusually handsome."

"'Cause he says women should have the right to vote!" He chuckled. "Suffragists see beyond a man's lack of physical appeal." He paused for dramatic effect. "God bless 'em!" He guffawed.

I laughed too. Then the sun began to rise, an exquisite, immense, orange-pink miasma spreading along the eastern slope like a slashed wrist oozing blood. We stayed quiet for a long time as we ascended the road leading up to Ophir Peak. The sky blossomed into a painted canvas, the illusion of being transported to another realm was acute.

Until Vestrick's claim came into view. In front of the tunnel was the menacing figure of big Bad Jace, glaring at us as we approached, his foul odor permeating my nostrils. The sun began to illuminate his position, and I noticed a large gunpowder fuse leading into the mine, where the quicksilver alcohol and nitric acid was stored. Bad Jace had a box of phosphorus matches in one hand, a Winchester rifle in the other.

I noticed, for the first time, that the mouth of the tunnel Vestrick had signed over to me pointed toward the sky, angled in the very direction that Grinaker intended to settle the air balloon.

Rosie's warning suddenly throbbed in my sleep-deprived brain.

The mountain is a gun.

27

I LEAPED OFF THE WAGON BEFORE SLEATH could bring it to a halt and went charging at Bad Jace, who smelled so wretched that I could've tagged him in total darkness. I could've shot him too, but the monster inside me needed to see him to suffer before he expired.

"Kid," he said. "Wait."

He blocked my first punch, a straight jab. My left hook though, hammered him flush on the ear. He yelped, staggered backward. Then I stepped forward again to throw a tremendous uppercut. My knuckle barely connected, catching the edge of his incisor, which speared my entire hand with a lacerating pain. He touched his upper lip and looked at his fingers, which were bloody. I jiggled the ache from my hand and saw I'd cut it badly, and blood was trickling.

"Listen," Bad Jace wetly mumbled, raising his other hand to indicate that he didn't want to fight.

"To your dying breath," I said. Behind him, however, I saw the balloon rising into the air and heading toward us.

"Kid, we've got to knock that balloon out of the sky before the railroad station is bombed," Bad Jace growled. "And then we have to save the President."

"I suspected you," I said, "of working for the slimy Confederates. I see that I'm wrong now. You're simply an insane person."

My statement was punctuated by a sudden, terrible detonation.

Bad Jace turned away from me to grab his field glasses from the saddle of his horse. I took the opportunity to smash his head with a rock. He fell to one knee but didn't lose consciousness.

I ripped the binoculars from him and assessed the approaching balloon.

The balloon's gondola contained Grinaker, his gun drawn on President Lincoln, and on someone that I never wanted to see floating a thousand feet in the air for any reason, under any conditions.

Ezra the shoeshine boy.

I smelled Bad Jace and heard him growl before he tackled me to the ground, sending the field glasses flying off the precipice of Ophir Peak and into the valley below. He had me clenched in a half nelson, using his disgusting legs to scissor my face and neck, locking me in place and preventing me from moving. His unwashed clothes were so revolting that I nearly passed out from the rancid odor rather than the crushing weigh of a 300-pound man pinning me.

"Ready to listen, Kid?"

"I'm ready," I said.

He released me and rolled away quickly, knowing full well that I might try to rabbit punch him.

"Do you see now?"

"Not exactly," I said, rubbing my wrenched jaw. "Explain your madness."

"Look!" Sleath shouted, still sitting in his mule wagon with his own field glasses.

Bad Jace and I watched as Ezra, threatened with a gun, dropped what looked like a small cannonball from the gondola. The object whistled as it fell. It landed near a division of US marshals and Pinkerton agents in pursuit, clipping three or four of them and their horses with shrapnel. The detonation rattled Mount Davidson, Ophir Peak trembling beneath our feet. The Marshals and Pinks that were still on their horses lifted their rifles to the sky and fired, trying to carefully put holes in the silk canvas and bring down the balloon. The distance was too great, however.

"Help me, Kid!" Bad Jace said, urging me to follow him to a piece of tarp-covered equipment. "Grinaker's going to blow up the railroad line to sabotage the Union!"

I ran over, and together we yanked the cover from what looked like another hydrogen machine.

"This can't be happening," I said.

Bad Jace pulled a lever. There was the sound of hissing gas, and a patch of silk canvas began expanding. The oafish, smelly bastard had somehow constructed another air balloon.

As the envelope inflated, it began catching a gritty breeze from the east and heading west toward Virginia City and the railroad station, the gondola being dragged to the edge of the cliff.

"Idiot!" I said. "You didn't tether the gondola!"

"Shut up and jump!" Bad Jace screamed back at me.

"Do you know how to pilot the balloon!"

"Of course not!"

"Lord, I pray mightily to thee," Sleath said within earshot.

Bad Jace tossed the old timer the box of phosphorus matches. "When Grinaker's balloon starts heading this way, light that gunpowder fuse."

Sleath nodded, eyes wide, anxious. He seemed to have become, to his dismay, sober.

From Grinaker's blimp, another bomb whistle-dropped and exploded.

"Do it, Kid!" Bad Jace screamed, as the wind picked up, blowing dust into our eyes and mouths.

Our balloon was now airborne, the gondola several feet from the precipice. Bad Jace started running first, and I followed, both of us leaping into sky and crashing into each other as we landed awkwardly inside the wicker basket.

Bad Jace stood up, turned a dial that pumped gas into the dirigible, increasing our elevation. We caught an air current going in the right direction, and off we went, hurtling toward Grinaker, Lincoln, and poor little Ezra.

We caught too much speed, it turned out. The gas-inflated, silk-shiny canvas of our craft collided mightily against Grinaker's balloon. We were slightly lower in elevation, so before we bounced away from our target, I managed to grab hold of Grinaker's valve cable, wresting it loose from the burner. I thought that, if I grounded my feet inside my gondola, I might keep Grinaker's balloon close and steady enough for Bad Jace to jump inside with Ezra and Lincoln.

That's not what happened. Instead, I was ripped from my own basket to find myself hanging by a cable from a balloon, a thousand feet in the sky and piloted by a gray-back sympathizer who, having kidnapped the President of the United States and my favorite shoeshine boy, was dropping bombs on the people and protectors of Virginia City.

Grinaker's aircraft snagged a different current and began heading faster toward Ophir Peak. I rope-climbed my way up the cable, which Grinaker hadn't yet realized was unfastened. He was struggling to work the unresponsive burner when I climbed into the gondola and punched him in the back of the head.

In an effort to help me, Lincoln vaulted at the Dead Dice owner, but since the basket suddenly shifted direction, he lurched, toppled, and ended up knocking into me, tangling us up. Now Grinaker had the advantage, pointing his pistol at me.

By this time, Ezra had climbed onto the basket's edge and jumped, grabbing the skirt of the balloon that hung above and outside the burner. He swung around the edge of the gas flame to grab the rope that connected the basket to the envelope, then used both feet to kick the gun in Grinaker's outstretched hand.

The pistol discharged, missing me but snapping one of the other basket connectors, sending Ezra and me plummeting from the sky.

To my amazement, we landed atop Bad Jace's balloon, cushioned within the deflation port. Our weight slowly caused the dirigible to lose elevation, gliding our way to the ground.

Hot air from the slightly ajar balloon gores warmed Ezra and me, nestled together in the pocket of our parachute vent. I held the little guy close, hoping that, if we hit the earth too hard, my body might cushion his little bones on impact.

I could sense Bad Jace's basket skidding along the high desert floor until we eventually came to a stop. The top of the balloon that we'd fallen into was stretched nearly twenty yards from the basket. Bad Jace ran over, swatting away the hiss-flattening load-tapes to reach us.

"That was," Bad Jace said, smiling, "nearly too much fun."

"Again!" Ezra cheered, juiced up on adrenaline.

Bad Jace's face quickly dropped, however, when he looked up toward Ophir Peak to see Grinaker trying to land the balloon on a cliff mesa beside Vestrick's mine, with Lincoln still in it.

"Sleath, my god. No."

The fuse had been lit.

There was a terrible, teeth-rattling explosion that sent a staggering amount of debris avalanching outward. Rocks, flying like cannonballs blasted from the field gun, shredded the balloon, and battered the basket and the bodies inside it.

We watched the carnage with feelings of utter dread and despondency. The mercury-powered blast untethered the gondola and ignited the burner gas, generating a powerful fireball in the heavens that outshone the Nevada sun.

We ran for cover to avoid getting hit by the falling wreckage. But where we ran wasn't much better and didn't offer us shelter from the storm of pent-up rage that had stewed in grayback conspirators for the last twenty-four hours in Virginia City. Nearly a dozen men on horses surrounded us. One carried a Confederate flag, the Stars and Bars. Half of the sympathizers were miners, their wives having tried to poison Lincoln the day before. The other half I recognized as being veterans of the two Pyramid Lake Indian War battles against the Paiutes. They'd become secessionists after being abandoned by a government that had sent them here to fight.

"That there's the Kid," a Confederate said.

"He looks ten years old," another said.

"Not the *little* kid. He's the shoeshine boy. I mean the *big* Kid. Kid Crimson."

"He looks like hammered coyote scat," another critiqued.

"That's what happens when you crash-land an air balloon," the second one said.

"He has lost," yet another observed, "that fresh new gunfighter smell."

"Let's put him and Bad Jace out to pasture," said the first Confederate. "Kill the young'un, too."

They raised their pistols. For the first time in my life, I had nothing with which to return fire. I summoned the most hateful expression I could muster.

Suddenly, a volley of lead sent seven of the men off their horses and into the dust, where they choked on their own blood.

There was the sound of a happy coyote pup. A cavalry of aggressive friends had arrived. Snake, the Cutter, Estrella, and her warrior-doves came galloping at full tilt, Winchesters cracking.

The remaining Confederates turned tail, riding away as fast as they could go, leaving Bad Jace, Ezra, and me unscathed.

Snake reached us first and laughed. "Tiny, your woman Poppy came to us with news of your big battle against the plot to kill President Lincoln. I hope that I don't run into him, because I will have to kill him on sight by using this—my father's bow and arrow."

Bad Jace opened his mouth to say something, but then thought better of it.

Causing everyone to flinch, two bodies abruptly crashed to the ground like sacks of burned, granulated potatoes.

Snake looked up to determine if any more corpses were raining down. Seeing none, he examined the two that were smashed into the dirt and said to me: "That one is Lincoln."

"Yes," I said.

Snake slotted an arrow, pulled back the string, and released, the arrow striking Lincoln dead in the chest.

Everyone was quiet and contemplative.

Finally, Estrella said, "Virginia City has nothing on Rattlepeak."

28

THE US ARMY COMMANDER AT FORT CHURCHILL
had been tasked by President Lincoln to probe the
strength of Southern sympathizers in Virginia City.
Turned out that it was significant. With the nation
stripped of troops to fight the Civil War, the Territory of
Nevada was left exposed. Everyone realized the value
that Nevada silver would have to the Southern cause and
what a disaster it would be to the Union if that resource
were lost to secessionists. Keeping the wealth from
Nevada mines in the hands of the Union was a top
priority.

That's why Orion Clemens and Ralston had devised a
plan to lure, out in the open, Confederate sympathizers.
The way to do that was to bring a body double of
Abraham Lincoln to town. Whoever participated in a plot
to kill him would be imprisoned, tried, and executed.
There were a lot of people arrested, indicted for insurrec-
tion, and transported to Fort Churchill for trial.

But the ringleader, Grinaker, the man who brought air
balloons to Virginia City and sought to make our town a

Confederate stronghold, was dead, killed by the gun that Bad Jace had installed on the side of a mountain. He smelled terrible, but he had a terrific imagination. I had unfairly dismissed him as a brute, when he was, in actuality, a connoisseur of weapons. Regarding the arsenic, Roscoe had confused Butenhoff for Bad Jace.

The Lincoln body double, poor soul, was a US Army Brigadier General named Reuben Tanner from Cleveland, Ohio. Grover did a sensational job reconstructing what was left of the patriot and displaying him inside First Presbyterian that Sunday. People came from as far as Cedar City, Utah, to say goodbye to the man who, for a brief and shining moment, brought light and joy and good feelings to a place mired in the muck of money and booze and rough trade.

Poppy and I took Ezra and Sarah to say farewell to the ersatz Honest Abe. We donned our fanciest duds and waited in line for an hour to pay our respects. We were taken aback by the outpouring of emotion that greeted Reuben Tanner. Indeed, Virginia City sent the Great Emancipator off into the Great Unknown with love in our hearts and tears in our eyes. We'd never seen anything like it, and we never would again.

No more balloons flew in the sky above Ophir Peak. Verbena bought the Dead Dice for a song, making the joint even more successful, more profitable than Grinaker. Chaparral didn't get his big break performing a piano concert for Lincoln. Grover had taken photographs of us standing next to a man impersonating the real president, who all along had been in Washington, DC, thousands of miles away. Grover had plenty of coffins in which to bury the dead, thanks to the order that the federal government had put in weeks earlier. The children didn't really eat lunch with the man who liberated the slaves. It was all a dream, and everyone returned to being our usual, mediocre, uninspired selves.

Except for Ezra and Sarah. Since he'd taught Sarah to shine shoes for the opera house celebration, they were soon operating two stands in Virginia City. Business picked up too, and the more our boomtown boomed— the more people came here to strike it rich, to change their lives, to find a vein of silver and new identity at the edge of the world, the last vestige of the frontier—the lighter our hearts felt as we counted our money and dreamed of our escape. We imagined our lives in a greener, saner place, where bloodshed was a memory and love a routine magic and salve.

WATCH FOR: THE GUNS OF GOBLIN VALLEY (KID CRIMSON 2)

After the Union Army's failed attempt to prosecute Confederate sympathizers in town, Kid Crimson is recruited by President Lincoln's intermediaries to scout a Mormon foundry suspected of manufacturing war materiél in Utah.

Kid makes the journey alongside Nellie Brown, a deadly knife-thrower he met at a traveling circus, saving a Latter-day Saints bruiser named Rocker Portwell from an Indian attack. The devout enforcer reveals the Mormons are building cannons for Lincoln, and together, they devise a plan to transport the weapons to Kansas.

But when the foundry is ravaged in a surprise assault by the cunning Rebel commander Prince Polignac, Kid must face a grim truth: Polignac aims to steal gold from Utah's secret Union bank and bring mercenaries and cannons to Virginia City, destroying the mines and slaughtering residents.

Kid Crimson won't back down. With Nellie's blades, a circus lion guarded by a 10-year-old Paiute animal whisperer, and an African elephant armored in Rocker's steel, he's ready to face Prince Polignac head-on.

Can his ace crew outmaneuver Polignac's forces and save Virginia City before it's too late?

AVAILABLE AUGUST 2024

ABOUT THE AUTHOR

Jarret Keene is an assistant professor in the Department of English at UNLV, where he teaches American literature and the graphic novel. He is the series editor for Las Vegas Writes, published by Huntington Press, and is the author of *Hammer of the Dogs*, and the middle grade books *Decide and Survive: The Attack on Pearl Harbor* and *Heroes of World War II: 25 True Stories of Unsung Heroes Who Fought for Freedom*. Keene has been interviewed by *Writer's Digest*, *Publisher's Weekly*, *EcoTheo Review*, *Library Thing*, *Black Fox Literary Magazine*, and Coast to Coast AM.

ABOUT THE AUTHOR